L. C. SON

Beta Rising: A Beautiful Nightmare Story

First published by L.C. Son Books 2022

Copyright © 2022 by L. C. Son

This novel is entirely a work of fiction. The names, characters and incidents portrayed in it are the work of the author's imagination. Any resemblance to actual persons, living or dead, events or localities is entirely coincidental.

First edition

ISBN: 979-8-9862237-0-4

*This book was professionally typeset on Reedsy.
Find out more at reedsy.com*

Contents

BETA
RISING
A BEAUTIFUL NIGHTMARE STORY
L.C. SON

Dedication

To everyone who survived the last two years.
To everyone who lost loved ones.
To everyone who witnessed the rise of turmoil, hate, sickness,
and pain.
Know you're not in this alone.
Keep going.
Find your pack.
And always know, no matter what… we rise and
fall… ***together***.

~ L.C. Son ~

A Note from L.C. Son

Dear Reader,

Thank you for choosing to read Beta Rising! I hope you enjoy it.

While Beta Rising is a standalone book in the Beautiful Nightmare series, I wholeheartedly recommend that you read other books in the series as your time allows. To aid in your understanding of the supernaturals and their hierarchy within the series, I've included a legend on the next page. It should give a little spoiler-free insight into the Beautiful Nightmare universe as you go through the story.

Please also note, Beta Rising contains mature content not suitable for those under 18. While not erotic, this book contains steamy situations, pillow talk, and some explicit language. Themes such as grief, loss, death, and some violence against supernatural and mortal characters are also discussed in detail. Readers with sensitivities to any of the above should consider these themes prior to proceeding with reading the book.

Again, I thank you for your interest in my beautifully nightmarish world. I truly hope you love it! Be sure to connect with me on Facebook, Instagram, and my website. I enjoy engaging with my readers. You can also sign up for my newsletter to stay up to date with all of my comings and goings. I've also curated a nice Beta Rising playlist on Spotify just for you! Use my link below to connect and groove with me.

https://linktr.ee/l.c.son

Dream Well,

L.C.

Supernatural Legend

BEAUTIFUL NIGHTMARE UNIVERSE
Supernatural Legend

ALTRINION

First born of Earthborn Supernaturals. Strength of the wind, earth, sky and strengthened by the sun. Ability to read mortal minds. Death only by obsidian blade or self-sacrifice through the Sacred Waters.

ALTRINION-VAMPIRES

Cursed by the blood of mortals once a mortal life is taken and forever destined to crave the humans they were bound to watch over. Cursed never to walk in the light of the sun; unless by selfless love they redeem their soul. Progenitor of all mortal-made vampires Death by Obsidian blade or the Sun

SCOURGE VAMPIRES

Mortal made; not of the Order of Altrinion Cursed by blood; savage and bloodthirsty. Commands power of the sky. Death by the Sun, decapitation, or mortal wound

CHANGELING

First born of Non-Earthbound Supernaturals. Powers of darkness, wind, and shadow. Cursed to a formless void after rebellion of the Order. Death only by a blade dipped in the Sacred Waters. Changeling jinn Bound by Keepers of the Order to golden jars of clay; destined to oblige the masters of their keep May only reclaim form through sacrificial procreation of earthbound souls; mortal and supernatural alike

HARBINGERS & PRAESIDIUM

Remnants of the world long past. Bulwarks, Gargoyles, Dragons, Deities and Gorgons. Relegated to both Earthbound and the dark world. Watch keepers & Gatekeepers.

WOLVES

Earthbound Lycan kin. Grand protectors of the Order.

PRIME & OMEGA WOLVES

Non tertiary of lunar ascendancy. Primes hold purview of Dunes, Pack, and all other wolfen-kind. Not subject to lunar cycle; may change at will. Omega holds purview of all. Titular ascendants with power over all animal and earthbound creatures of nature.

PACK & DUNES WOLVES

Bound to the manner of lunar succession; Pack wolves are cursed to shift only at full moon. Dunes wolves also at the mercy of the moon, with exception to alphas & primes.

THE CURSE OF SKULL WOLVES

By the order of Altrinion, all earthbound will abide by the form of man. Walking this earth in his likeness and stature, wolves of lunar succession must not be found unmated, deserted, barren, or lacking earthbound affinity or mammon. Dereliction is akin to apostasy. Wolves forgone as such break the bonds of succession and kinship of MAN; forever cursed to a hollowed, soulless form. A skull. A desolate monstrosity.

Introduction

Not like this. Who would author such a short and tragic love story? Certainly not me. This is not what I envisioned when I took Braelyn in my arms for the first time.

After spending the better part of my adolescence pining over the one vampire girl who initially regarded me as a playboy only to herself fall for my wolfish wiles, we should have had more time together.

Braelyn Agatha Dortches. Or the B.A.D. goth-girl, as everyone referred to her.

She was the one I wasn't supposed to love. But I did. And she loved me. She loved me so much she gave up her vampirism for me, making herself human. All so that she could be with me, an alpha, become my wife, and ensure my bloodline.

We never made it to the altar.

I should've listened to Brian. He knew it would never work. He knew as I now understand, any pledge to the blood of a Changeling can cost you your very life. Us wolves have known this since the day a Changeling's lure fooled the progenitor of our pack, Orion, in the old days. It was the trickery of the Changelings that marked the Dunes wolves in a cursed pack. A curse that should have ended with me. I swore an oath to my den I'd not allow it to rule my pack ever again.

But here I sit, riddled in a cloud of sorrow, regret, and anger.

Deep fears brew within me, knowing I only have until the next cycle of the full moon to ensure I fulfilled my oaths to the elders.

Who would have thought when we bonded the Changeling's pledge to Damina's life as a proxy to Braelyn, that Damina Nicaud, of all people would enact her Altrinion curse, by killing a human, becoming an Altrinion-Vampire herself would nullify Braelyn's newly human life? Not me. Not even Braelyn.

No one.

If there was anyone who never had a murderous bone in their body, it was the Lady Damina Nicaud. But everyone has their limits. And Damina met hers. Seeing her aunt struck down by the treacherous betrayal of her once dearest friend, Allyson, I cannot blame Damina for striking a blow straight to Allyson's heart.

Yet, inasmuch as I understand Damina's reasons, it was not only Allyson's heart who she crushed. It was my beloved Braelyn.

My Braelyn. The woman who should have sealed my heart forever brought about my heart's end.

Now, I'm left with nothing but madness, rage, and a big oath to fulfill. An oath heavier than even the pain of my heart. And if I don't rise to meet the challenge, my people will fall.

So I'll tuck my heart deep in the dark casing of my soul, knowing it'll take more than a scythe to pry it out.

Chapter 1

"He'll come out when he's ready!" I hear Brian bark from outside my bedroom suite. He's been posted at my door nearly every day since that day. With exception to the times he runs off to check on Dacari, he's never more than a stone's throw from me.

More surprising is that neither Cal nor Bessie have sought to throw me out of their tavern. I'm sure they could use the money they'd normally get from renting out a room. But I can't pry myself from the last place I spent with her.

Everything in this room reminds me of her. This was the last place I held Braelyn in my arms. This is where we kissed for the last time. This is where we stared at the shadow of the moon beyond the tree line and rehearsed our vows.

Vows we were meant to say just after Damina and Jackson said their I do's. Vows that never came for either of us.

Once Allyson's treacherous body fell to the ground, a loud, shrilling cry erupted from Damina as her cursed form took over. Screaming in agony and smitten with grief, she took flight before Jackson could console her or convince her otherwise.

Both the sight of her aunt's fallen state and the killing of Allyson were already too much to take in. But when she saw how her actions affected Braelyn, as I carried my lifeless betrothed down the hall, she fled.

I don't blame her.

A part of me wishes I could take flight and flee the place of my pain, but it's been two weeks and I can barely pry myself from this place.

I can still smell her.

Queens & Monsters. The Henry Rose perfume Braelyn wore melted into every fabric, bed linen, and even the window dressing. That's just how Braelyn did life. She permeated everything. She was everywhere.

She was everything.

She still is.

"He has a duty to the pack!" Gregory roars back, and I can almost feel the oak shutters of my windows rattle.

"How dare you!" Brian snaps and I hear a loud thump against my door. It doesn't take a genius to know someone just got shoved. Not surprising. There's no love lost between the two gaudy Goliaths outside my suite. They're both in love with the same woman. Dacari Peyroux. That will prove to be a mess in its own making, but not one that I choose to become involved.

I'm the last person who needs to meddle with anyone's heart.

I know I should go out and stop them, but I barely have the mental fortitude to do so.

Maybe it's because it all happened so fast. Or perhaps it's because I never got closure.

Since she was bound by the Changeling pledge, her body lit aflame once Damina's curse took root. So we had no body to bury. Her only family was Dalcour. She had no other family to mourn her beyond me. Dalcour did what he does best when the pain becomes too much, return to his monstrous vampire self. Upon hearing the news of both Damina and Braelyn's state, he carried his rage into the city, running a rampage of carnage through New Orleans.

At one point, Brian gave me the daily body count through the door, but after the number hit beyond a hundred, he stopped telling me.

We've all been privy to Dalcour's ravenous bouts throughout the years, but this is by far the worst. On the one hand, he lost Damina to Jackson and the Altrinion curse in less than twenty-four hours, and on the other, he lost my beloved, the one he considered somewhere between a little sister and daughter. Not to mention seeing the factions of vampires falling to the lure of his wretched brother Decaux, I hardly expect Dalcour to have anything left in him to mourn.

So here I sit alone in my grief, inhaling the faint scent of her perfume as it wanes day after day.

Reminiscing on our last night together, I still regret we never made love. Although we did everything else under the moonlight, we wanted to wait until we made it official before we took that ultimate step.

Stupid, I know.

One rule of wolf mating with an outsider, they must be able to withstand the power of the wolf's mating call and imprinting. While it's risky for humans, we were certain the power of the Changeling within Braelyn would give her the fortitude to endure the mating.

Now we will never know.

What's worse is that being an only son of an only son, all the weight of continuing my bloodline rests with me. I pledged my bloodline as an oath to the elders to strip away the Dunes curse of the moon. If I don't find a mate soon, my pack will once again be bound by the moon, forced to shift at its mercy. Not only that, but if we are once again accursed, then our power as Beta Prime, second in command of wolfen kind, and guardians of the supernatural world, will be stripped away.

As newly appointed Alpha of the Beta Primes, it is my responsibility to ensure the Dunes wolves maintain not only our hierarchy but also never be subjected to such a curse ever again.

It's a boulder of a weight for someone whose heart is shredded in two. Still, I know somehow, I cannot sulk in my sullen state for long.

Once more, loud thumping sounds bang against my door, slowly lulling me away from my grief.

"Both of you, stop it!" A fierce, grisly growl bellows from outside my suite.

"My Lord, I told this imbecile it's time for these puppies to get their sh—"

"That will be enough, Gregory!" I now make out Jackson's grumbling rebuke.

Slowly pulling myself up from where I've planted myself from the floor at the foot of the bed, I wipe the dust from my pant legs. Wobbling as I do, I force a quick look in the mirror. I haven't looked at myself in weeks and though I hardly care to do so now, I'd hate for my Prime Alpha to see me in such a sunken state. Although I suspect he looks far from fetching with his recent loss of Damina, I know too well how wolves, Prime wolves in particular, frown upon being unkempt.

With my eyes barely cracked, I can hardly make out the man staring back at me. A wooly mane and gruff beard cover most of my face, barely allowing my usually bright bluish-green eyes their normal shimmer. I even try to force a willful shine of my typical sun-spun wolfen eyes, but to no avail. I suspect my wolf is also done with me.

I can't blame him. I'm reeking!

I haven't bathed in days.

Not that my own smell doesn't offend me, but I'm still covered in Braelyn's ashen remains. I just can't bring myself to wash it off. The thought of doing so pains me.

So despite the looks I'll likely get from the pack, or my Prime Alpha, for that matter, they'll all just have to deal.

I really don't care.

Before I can pull myself away from the mirror, holding myself up by gripping the crackling walnut oak and wicker dresser, the door swings open. The light from the hallway stings my eyes as the sliver of sunlight beams inside my suite from the hall windows. Using my forearm as a shade, I gaze at Jackson's large, stately presence illumining my door as if an aura of light hovered over the entirety of his massive frame.

He takes small steps inside. Almost too small for a man his size, but I've learned enough about Jackson to know he's trying to not only be patient but considerate of my feelings.

Feelings, I'm sure to which he can relate.

Still, as he makes his way beyond the threshold, I am surprised to find him more well-kept than I would think to find him. His long brunette mane is groomed and pulled into a ponytail. As his face comes into view, I spy his meticulously etched goatee as well as detect a whiff of his brash, woody scent as a small smile curves the corners of his lips.

What does he have to be happy about? Has he found Damina?

Is she safe? Did they get married?

If so, why would Brian neglect to tell me? *What the fu —*

"Hello, Young Alpha," Jackson's gentle words slice through my thoughts. His tone is softer than I expected it to be, but still typical of his demeanor.

"My Lord," my voice crackles in a whispered reply as my eyes sheepishly wander to the floor, taking notice of his careful steps toward me.

"My Lord Helsing, if you're not ready for this—" Brian begins and I raise my hand in caution, still keeping my gaze low in submission. Brian grumbles as I do but affixes himself at the threshold of my door. Without looking up, I also notice a second shadow at the door, and I'm certain Gregory is lurking behind Brian.

"Leave us," Jackson barks over his shoulder, his irritation with Brian clear.

Brian groans in response, but drags the door shut. "I'll be right here," he affirms as the door closes. Jackson sighs heavily as he does, obviously annoyed by Brian's would-be threatening tone, but forces his hands in his pockets and leans against the wall.

With the door now closed, the room is dark. Too dark for our shared liking, and Jackson quickly flicks the light switch on, causing my eyes to flinch at the beaming bright LED lights blaring from the wall sconces on either side of the wall. Pinching my nose as my only recourse until my eyes adjust, I force my grumbling aside. If anyone but my Prime Alpha turned that light on, I'd rip their arms from their body.

"I'm sorry, Mark. I know the light is bright," Jackson begins, resuming his caring tone. "But I think we both know it's far time for you to step into the light."

At his words, my eyes slowly trail up the length of him, taking special notice of his creased gray trousers and fitted black shirt. How the hell he maintains appearances during a time like this is beyond me. Unless things are truly better for him than they seem. I can only wonder.

Half-heartedly, I try to curve my lips into a smile, but I haven't smiled in weeks and the dry edging of my skin instantly cracks at my failed attempt. Tasting my own blood isn't something I enjoy, but it strangely awakens my wolf and a low grumble churns deep through my chest as Jackson and I slowly lock eyes.

"That's it, Young Alpha. It's time to awake. Listen to your wolf. He's ready. Waiting." Jackson's words are more an order despite his gentle tone. One thing is for sure, my wolf hears him.

Another low growl settles in my chest, and I feel my wolf flexing beneath my skin like one awakening from a long slumber. Heaving hard as the pacing of my heart quickens, I know my wolf is indeed heeding his alpha's call. And even if I wanted to, there is nothing I can do to stop him.

Jackson's stance widens and I hear a low snarl rumble through him as well. Lifting my eyes slightly, the golden flash of his gaze locks with my own, and I instantly feel more aware than I've felt in the weeks since Braelyn's death.

As though new life was breathed in my nostrils, I feel a strangely intense fervor at my alpha's call and it's like a defibrillator to my weakened heart. Issuing one more roar, I distinctly hear my name within the cadence of his cowl. Growling in return, I feel my muscles flex as my eyes brighten, causing me to see Jackson's wolf peering at me beyond the hazy view of his mortal form.

Shocked, I take a step back. I've never seen that in another wolf before.

"What—what my lord was that?" I stutter, taking hold of the chest of drawers at my side.

Blaring his typical kind smile, his eyes seem to smile back at me. Letting out a small laugh, Jackson's eyes return to their normal hue. "You are an alpha now, Mark. Everything will look differently from now on."

Chapter 2

Stuffing one of his hands in his pocket, he saunters past me and pulls the cord on the terrace shade. I squint as he does. Just the sliver of sunlight peering in through the drapes is almost too much. Especially since I haven't seen the sun in weeks.

"It's time we let in a little light; don't you think?" Jackson smiles, twisting the cord on the other side of the terrace. I want to tell him to keep it closed, but he's my Prime Alpha and no matter how kind he may appear, I know better than to test his resolve. "Don't worry, Young Alpha, the sun will set soon, so it won't be bright for long."

Pulling the small armchair from the side table near the terrace, it scrapes against the floor and the sound pierces my ears like nails on a chalkboard. Even my hearing seems more sensitive than before.

"I guess that's just the way things are sometimes," he begins as he sits down, folding one leg over his knee.

Walking over to the bed to sit across from him I feel like perhaps I missed a part of the conversation. Maybe his words got muddled when he scraped the floor with the chair. "My lord? What things are you referring to?"

"Remain standing!" He quickly orders me just before my butt

hits the bed cushion. There's a low snarl bellowing between his words, and I know he means it.

Chucking my legs together, I square my shoulders, but lowering my head slightly. I never had to deal much with wolf polity coming up. My father was too busy chasing women to give me much guidance. I learned much of what it means to be a wolf from Lord Marchand, his Guard trainer, Dranoel, and Brian. Brian taught me a lot, but being an orphaned wolf himself, even what I got from him was like putting puzzle pieces together. Everything else I know I've learned on the fly, or by instinct.

And my instinct tells me, just toe the line. The good thing is, towing the line isn't hard with Jackson. He's fair. Although Brian isn't sold on him, I've always been a good judge of character and I know Jackson means me no harm.

"Yes, my lord," I dutifully reply, gathering my hands at my back.

"Relax your hands at your sides, young one," Jackson barks, lowering his leg back to the ground. He shifts around in his seat a bit before clasping his hands together, resting them beneath his chin as he regards me. "Now please, sit."

I glance up at him, hopeful I heard him right. Nodding with his eyes and a small smile at the corner of his mouth, he affirms once more before I sit.

"As an alpha it is important your den knows to adhere to your word, and your word alone. Do you understand?"

"Yes, my lord." Ahh—a teaching moment. My heart thumps thankful.

"And always—always—see what a man has in his hands. Especially those in your charge. Don't let yourself be caught by surprise. It's better to see the knife before it stabs you in the back. Do you understand?"

"Yes, my lord. Thank you."

Tightening his clasped hands, he smiles once more. "But you can relax with me."

No sooner than he finishes his sentiment, the tension in my shoulders fades. I've been a statue since he arrived. I didn't realize how tense I'd become, but I'm glad he noticed.

"Listen, Mark, I understand how you feel—you know I do. But the sun is going down and soon the night will awaken. We can no longer sit back idly as the havoc wreaked upon us all goes unchecked. No matter how heartbroken we are."

I frown. "Sir?" What havoc is he talking about?

Gazing down at me, his brows tighten. "Are you telling me you have no idea what's going on?"

Crap. This won't go well. This is my city, and I should know what's going on.

"Has no one told you? Not even Brian?" I only turn my head slightly before he jumps from his seat. I rise as he does, but he motions his hand downward. "Sit down!" Jackson orders me and turns to peek out of the terrace window. "This—this is totally unacceptable!"

"I'm sorry, my lord. I know I've let my grief—"

"No! None of this is on you, young one. It's all on me."

Straightening my posture, I want to stand and assure him he's done nothing wrong, but I know better and remain seated. "My lord, this is not your fault. This is my city and you charged me to protect it. Whatever havoc taking place is mine to blame."

Tightening his lips and quickly relaxing to a smile, Jackson lets out a sigh and falls back to his chair. "While I appreciate your sentiment, Lord Helsing, do remember, I am your Prime

Alpha. And as your Prime, the totality of every city is under my purview. I knew you were grieving. I should not have assumed you knew what was going on. It was my job to ensure you knew. But I did not. I assumed. And an alpha cannot make an assumption. An alpha must know. Because when we assume things, we quite literally make an ass out of ourselves every time. I, more than anyone, know this to be true. Yet, I continue to make an ass out of myself time and time again."

Leaning back into the chair, Jackson sighs hard again, closing his eyes tight.

I wish there was something I could say to help him, but I am at a loss for words. One would think by looking at him, he had it all together, but as strange as it seems, he appears just as lost as I am.

"Well, let it be a lesson to you not to be an ass," he laughs, seemingly annoyed with himself. "Quite frankly, had I not been an ass in the way I handled things with Damina, none of this might not be going on right now." His words trail, and it's as though I got a sneak peek into his inner monologue. I'm not sure I was supposed to hear what he just said.

"My lord," I begin, averting his attention back to me when I see his eyes glare off into the distance. "How can I help you? What would my alpha have me do?"

Quickly, Jackson sits up right, relaxing his hands at his sides. "Thank you, Lord Helsing," he smiles. "But please know I understand what you've been going through. Losing Braelyn the way you did—no one should have to endure such pain."

A thick lump swells in my throat and my eyes sting as tears threaten to glass my view of Jackson's kind eyes. "Thank you, my lord. But the same can be said of you. Damina—I mean Lady Nicaud, she—"

Lifting his hand to stop me from continuing, "It's quite all right, Mark. When Damina saw what happened to Braelyn it destroyed her. More than even you or I can understand. And as hard as it is for me to move on, I know I must. I am an Alpha first. As are you."

Sucking in a breath, I nod. "Yes, my lord." I can tell it hurts him to talk about her. But I still need more. "It's just—and I hope I don't offend you." I wait for Jackson to give me the go ahead to continue. He affirms with his eyes only, and I go for it. "How are you not a wreck? How are you still moving forward?"

Once more, Jackson allows a small smile. "Because I must. It's what we do. As alpha's we must rise above even our own will for the good of our pack. For the good of all. I love Damina with every fabric of my being, but I have a duty as an alpha. And I know when it's all said and done that even in my dutifulness as alpha, my actions also help her. Sure she may not understand it now—hell, if I understand it all myself—but what I do, or rather what we do as alphas is for the good of all."

Damn, this guy is too good to be true. I almost want to be him when I grow up. There's not a frigging selfish bone in his perfectly Prime Alpha body.

"Don't get me wrong," he huffs. "It's not easy. I mean, I'm no better than the next man. All I want is to have my woman in my arms, love the hell out of her, and make her forget all the cares of the world. And why?"

"Because we love to protect, and *we protect what we love.*"

I smile as Jackson joins in unison as I echo the Pack Pledge. If I learned nothing else about being a wolf, those words were etched in my brain since I was a pup.

"That's right, young alpha," he laughs. "So now you know why I'm here."

Shrugging my shoulder, my head bobs to the right. "My lord?"

"It is our job to protect and to love. But I can't expect you to do that in your current state. And as much as I need your help with the fallout of the mess of the Marchands and Dacari, I need your head clear."

"Hold on, my lord. What do you mean the mess of the Marchands? And Dacari?"

"Well, after losing Braelyn and Damina, Dalcour is out of control. But Decaux has vowed to help us rein in his brother. It's the least he could do after everything he and Dacari have done."

"Okay, I knew about Dalcour. But what else have Decaux and Dacari done? I thought Dacari came here for Delia. I am so confused."

"Fine, I'll sum it up for you. Since she's teamed up with her wretched father, they've unleashed something upon this world that will take all of us combined to clean up. Whatever musings Decaux had her chant did not cure Scourge vampires as they first believed. Instead, it's turned anyone bitten into rabid monsters of some kind. We've done our best to contain the situation. But truly, I thought Brian told you."

"No, he didn't," I mumble. This is frustrating. Knowing how much Brian cares for Dacari, I don't know why he hasn't mentioned any of this to me.

"But I don't want you worrying about any of this. At least not yet."

"How can I not? It sounds like utter chaos. I've been so sunken in my grief, I've left you alone in this. For that, I apologize. What do you need me to do?" I say, jumping up from the bed. This time I'm not waiting for permission.

Lifting his hands in caution, he growls low. "Lord Helsing!" Stepping in front of me before I can make my way across the room, he catches my gaze. Growling once more, his wolf challenges mine to submit. I grimace, as I feel the weight of his will heavy upon my own.

Shit. I've never been put in submission like this before, but it sucks. It feels like someone arm wrestling your heart, making you cry uncle.

"Look Mark, I'm afraid until you get your head in the game, there's nothing you can do. Perhaps that's why Brian didn't tell you. But even then, that is not his decision to make. That's my call—and mine alone!"

Okay, so now it's all starting to make sense. Brian is stepping on Jackson's Prime Alpha toes. Although I'm not sure why Brian is being obstinate, it's clear enough to cause a rift between him and Jackson.

"Yes sir," I reply, lowering my eyes. I need Jackson to know I'll submit to him. Even if I don't understand everything. I trust him.

He stares on at me a bit, and I know he's ensuring I understand my place. I do. Even more, I have no desire to get in between him and Brian. B is like a brother to me, but Jackson is my alpha and I respect him.

"First and foremost, you still have an oath to fulfill. As alpha of the Beta Primes you promised to ensure your bloodline. Therefore you must find a mate."

And there it is. The one thing I knew would hit me like a wrecking ball in the gut is here and there's nothing I can do about it.

"Look, I know it's almost too soon to discuss, but—"

"I understand," I interrupt him. I know what happens next. They'll just round up someone for me to mate to ensure the bloodline. Hell, that's how I got here. My father wasn't in love with my mother. She was just the next wolf in line, suitable for an alpha. It's not what I would've wanted but it's what must happen.

Stunned, Jackson stares on at me with his lips parted, and I know I've done it now. I've left my alpha speechless.

Chapter 3

"*The copula ritual.*" My soft tone seems to come across as though I shouted. "Yep, that's how I was conceived." I admit, giving my Prime Alpha a little more insight into my life.

That's the problem with how things have been over the years. Us Dunes wolves have been left out of the traditional pack life for so long, most know little about us. Not even my Prime Alpha Jackson Nashoba. And while it sucks that it took our worlds colliding in the worst way possible, it does feel good knowing I can talk to him.

Perhaps the alpha primes aren't as self-centered as everyone has made them out to be.

"I see," Jackson groans, forcing his hand back in his pocket and pacing the floor once more. "I know what happened to your father. But what about your mother?"

Blowing out a heap of air, I force my hair from my face. Jackson's eyes search mine, and I know he senses how tough a topic this is for me, but he lifts his hand, shaking his head to acknowledge my pain.

"I'm sorry, Mark. You don't need to say anything more. I lost my mom when I was young too. My father died when I was a teen. So I understand."

"It's okay, my lord. I mean it still sucks, but I don't mind talking about it. Least of all to you. My mother left us. She hated my father. He wasn't good to her. Used her to conceive and then went about his life. Since she wasn't permitted to take me since I was next in succession, she left. I only saw her a few times after she left. But she died when I was eleven. Rogue hunters got her on a full moon. She was buried in our family plot. But my memory of her is hazy. At her funeral, though, my dad almost seemed contrite. For a minute I think he wished he treated her better. Still, it didn't last long. He went right back to his philandering ways."

Sighing, Jackson tilts his head toward me as he pats my shoulder. "Lord Helsing, you are a testament of one not easily broken by circumstance. The heart of the alpha beats strong in you. I knew that the day I met you just as clearly as I see it in your eyes now."

"Thank you, my lord," I answer, relieved. It feels good to share my life's pain with Jackson. Goodness knows I don't easily share much about myself with anyone.

"Are you completely sure you want to do this?" Jackson asks, his eyes still searching my face.

I want to tell him no, but what other options do I have? If I say no and find myself without a mate by the next full moon, my pack will be doomed. The Dunes Pack has had their share of challenges through the ages, but the last thing I want is for my name to be akin to Orion.

"Just as you've done my lord, I will put my duty to the pack above all. Whatever mate is chosen, I will abide with. I will not abandon her or lead a carnal life. I will remain a dutiful mate. Even more, I will lead those under my charge."

An appreciative smile covers Jackson's face but there remains a sadness minced in his smile that slightly troubles me.

"You do understand whatever mate is chosen, there is no return. And by the rights of the copula ritual, the sole purpose is for procreation. And who knows? One day you may even, perhaps love—"

"I won't." My blunt tone is intentional. Yes, he's my alpha, but even he knows it's too soon for me to think of love beyond Braelyn.

Jackson steps back, creating a bit of distance between us as he regards me. "Well, love your mate or not, you must procreate. But by rights the only means for choosing is scent. You'll not be allowed to see anything. Not her face, eyes, smile—anything."

"Yes, my lord. I understand."

"After your mate is selected, you'll make your way to an old den keep I just visited. You'll only have the allowable time of one week to mate. At the apex of the full moon, should you not have mated and imprinted, your alpha status will be revoked, and your pack forfeit. From it, the curse upon the Dunes Pack will return."

Jackson locks his eyes with mine and silence sits between us. I know he wants to know without a doubt that I understand what I'm agreeing to.

With my hands at my side, I dip my head once more in submission. Nodding in affirmation, Jackson sucks in a breath once more before squeezing my shoulder as he walks by me on his way to the door.

"I mean what I said, Lord Helsing, you are a true testament. Those in your charge are privileged to share pack soil with you, young alpha. And indeed, so am I." Jackson smiles once more before leaving quickly.

His feet are heavy as he walks down the hallway. With each

thump, I hear more feet scurry along the wooden floor.

Sitting back down at the side of my bed, I push my hair back from my face, thinking about what I just agreed to. I know it must be done, but it's not how I wanted things to go.

This should be me and Braelyn. Married. Happy. In love.

Not some archaic ritual made for the sole purpose of procreation. Although, I am appreciative such a tradition exists. I wouldn't be here without it.

Still, I wanted better for my life.

Now I'll have to truly be led by my nose.

They say when a wolf finds his mate, their pheromones mingle in the air and that's how a wolf chooses his mate. In our tradition, a wolf can either marry for love or mate for life. Sometimes it works out that a mate is also the one a wolf loves. But if not, it's a mate for life. I know some who fell in love with their mates over time.

Bessie and Cal were like that. Cal mated Bessie first, but she wanted to find love. When she didn't find love in the traditional sense, Cal was right there ready and waiting for her. In time, admiration grew to respect, and respect turned to love. Now they run this tavern together, helping wayward supernaturals, abused women, all under the guise of a wonderful restaurant right here in the French Quarter.

I can only hope to have such an ending.

But right now, I'm not looking for love. I'll simply settle for a mate.

"Have you lost your mind!" I hear Brian roar as he throws my door open.

The bright lights from the hall don't burn my eyes like they did before, but they still annoy me.

"B, close the door," I grumble, keeping my hands against my

forehead.

His large frame hovers in the doorway and it's the only thing keeping the light at bay. Mumbling something, he kicks the door behind him as he makes his way toward me.

"Seriously, Mark, don't tell me you fell for this copula bullsh—"

"Watch your tone, Brian!" I bark back and he leans away from me.

Keeping his hands to his side, he snarls in frustration, but I can tell he's working hard to control himself. "I'm sorry," he begins, lowering his head slightly. "It's just I don't understand why you'd want to put yourself through that ancient crap."

Standing, I watch Brian take a step back as he regards me warily. "Well, that crap is how I got here, B. You know this! Besides, what do you expect me to do? I can't very well sit here moping."

"Hell, Mark, for all I know it's how I got here too, but tradition be damned! You're still just as much an alpha if you have a mate or not! Name one wolf, from here to this side of the Mississippi capable of taking up the mantle as you have."

"What would you have me do, Brian? Stay in here sulking? Meanwhile the city I love is running about with rabid creatures of which you chose not to tell me about. Why? Is this because you were trying to protect Dacari?"

Brian's eyes flash bright gold and I know I hit a soft spot. I know he loves Dacari. I also know he's probably protecting her. Even from me.

"Maybe I'm also trying to protect you."

"How, B? By keeping me locked up in here? All I know is that I need to find a mate, so I can keep my alpha status as well as keep the Dunes out of the binds of that wretched curse. That's the only way I can do my part and lead my pack. *My pack, Brian. Not yours.*"

Brian's shoulders slump and he lowers his eyes. "Of course, my lord. I would never try to usurp your pack. I was only looking out for you. Quite frankly, I feared when you and Braelyn took on the Changelings pledge things would end like this. This isn't what I wanted for you."

"I know Brian. It's not what either of us wanted. But here we are. I can't let the pack fall into ruin. I just can't fail. Not again."

"You are no failure, my lord. There is no failure in you. Never has been."

Letting his eyes lift to mine for a minute, Brian allows a small smile to creep over his face. And as always, I see in his eyes what I've always seen. My friend.

"I couldn't agree more!" I hear Jackson merrily say from the threshold of my suite. "The Louisiana den and Beta Primes have quite a stout-hearted alpha."

Rolling his eyes, Brian sneers. "Indeed."

Narrowing my gaze slightly, I shake my head in caution. I need Brian to show more respect or at least muster a tinge of restraint where Jackson is concerned.

"My lord," I say, walking around Brian. I tug his arm a little, gesturing for him to turn around and face Jackson. "I was just letting Brian here know that he is to be under your charge as interim while I complete the rituals." I lie, but it's my way of moving the conversation along.

Brian steps to my side, gazing at me in shock as does Jackson. They both know what this means.

I've chosen Brian as my beta.

"Are you sure, Lord Helsing?" Jackson asks.

Peering over my shoulder, Brian's blue eyes grow wide. "You don't have to do this, Mark. I've got your back no matter what. I don't need to—"

"Yes, my lord," I smile again, patting Brian on the shoulder.

"Ah, so does your beta understand should you not meet your conditions, the charge of alpha falls to him?" Jackson says to me yet keeping his attention on Brian.

"I do. My lord," Brian answers, dragging his last words. "I will serve at your behest while my alpha attends to his duties in ritual. That is, of course, as long as I am permitted to ensure the safety of Dacari Peyroux."

Crap. Why did he have to bring up Dacari? Whatever mess she's gotten herself into seems to be where the problem lies.

"Of course!" Jackson replies in a tone brighter than I expected. "I know that is not only what Damina would want, but I wouldn't be able to keep you away from Dacari if I tried."

"Indeed, my lord," Brian adds.

Walking toward us, Jackson squares his shoulders, shooting a sharp eye to Brian. "But make no mistake about it, I care for Dacari like a sister. I've known her a lot longer than you. If at any point I suspect your sentiment toward her is anything less than she deserves, I'll have no problem ripping your head from your body and serving it to her devil of a daddy, Decaux myself."

Brian's eyes narrow back, but he keeps his expression restrained. "If I should ever do anything to hurt her, I would expect nothing less."

Groans stir between both Brian and Jackson as their eyes lock with one another. While I know Brian isn't posturing, I don't want him to come off as challenging our Prime Alpha.

That would be a mistake.

"Well," I work in a faux laugh, to break up their intense stare down. "I suppose we're all clear on Brian serving as my interim while I go through the ritual." Squeezing Brian's shoulder, I feel him relax beneath my palm and he takes a step back, creating space between him and Jackson.

Still, Jackson's posture remains stiff as he regards Brian. His eyes narrow and a low growl simmers through him.

It's a warning.

He needs Brian to know he will not be challenged. Brian affirms with his eyes lowered. I think he gets the point.

Chapter 4

Slowly, Jackson's posture relaxes, and he turns his attention back to me. I am thankful as I watch a small smile soften the rigid lock-jaw expression he had only moments ago.

"Well, everything is being arranged as we speak," Jackson announces in a brighter tone than before.

"Oh wow," I say under my breath. "That was fast."

"I know it seems that way," Jackson says as he leans against the doorpost. "But we've been preparing for this for a few days. I've had Sophie and Bessie gather a few potentials for you."

Surprised, I look behind me to Brian, who only tightens his mouth in response, still keeping his head low.

"Please, don't be upset with Brian," Jackson adds, once more raising his palm in caution. "In his defense he only found out a few days ago that I wanted to bring it up to you."

Hunching his shoulders in response, Brian cracks a weak smile. I know this isn't what Brian wanted for me, but we both know I have an obligation to the pack.

Lifting to the balls of my feet, attempting to match Jackson's ridiculous stature, I force another smile. "So potentials, eh?"

Smiling brightly in return, Jackson squeezes my shoulder.

"Yes, and if you can imagine, Sophie and Bessie have gathered none but the very best. Twelve in total."

"Twelve?" Damn. Where did he find these women? I shudder to think. "All wolves?"

"Most are wolves. There are a few hybrids and maybe a mortal or two."

"Mortals? Do we really want to go down that road?" I ask, thinking how bad things panned out for Braelyn.

Jackson's eyes fall and his lips tighten as he regards me. Gently patting my shoulder, he catches my gaze. "Look, I know what you must be thinking, but this is different. None of this will be orchestrated by Changeling witchery. No proxy needed. All of these women have been vetted."

"Meaning that they are fertile!" Gregory blurts.

Jackson turns to Gregory and issues a rebuking glare.

I'm no fan of Gregory. I haven't liked the guy since the first day we met, but I appreciate his candor. The last thing I need is for history to repeat itself.

"That's fine with me. I'm just finding a mate."

My offhanded remark doesn't sit well with either Jackson or Brian. I can tell Jackson is only doing this to ensure our pack remains intact. Brian wants better for me.

So do I.

But beggars can't be picky.

Brian takes a few steps closer, circling me a bit until he makes eye contact. "Mark, are you sure you want to do this? Maybe there's another way."

"It's okay, B. This is for the good of the pack. I've sat in here sulking long enough. Besides, if things are getting as bad out there as our Prime Alpha says, I have to be in position. The last thing we need is for our pack to rescind to the curse of the moon just when all hell breaks loose. I'd hate for that to happen because I didn't keep my oath. All I have to do is choose a mate."

"A mate for life." Brian whispers back, his eyes searching mine for indecision.

"Then a mate for life it will be." I exclaim, stepping forward.

An appreciative smile spreads across Jackson's face. He's proud of me. That means more to me than he thinks. I know Jackson has sacrificed more than any of us could imagine. So if he can stand strong, so can I.

"Well, first things first," Jackson begins as he walks toward the hallway. "You need to shower. At least make yourself somewhat presentable for your mate."

Crap. I hadn't thought about that. I'm still wearing Braelyn's ashes on me.

"Um, a shower, my lord? I'm ready now." I really don't want to let her go that easily.

Gregory taps Jackson's shoulder, and his attention turns behind him. Lifting a finger to Gregory, he turns back to me. "I know and I appreciate your willingness to get things going. But in order for this to work, your pheromones must match and mingle with that of your mate. We can't have your wolf confused by the varying scents you're carrying. Don't worry, we've had the potentials do the same."

Jackson turns to Gregory and mutters something to him and someone else in the hallway. As he does, the weight of his words rest heavy on me. How can I just wash what's left of Braelyn down the drain? Can I really do this?

Once more, stinging tears sit behind my eyes. Perhaps Brian is right. Maybe this is too soon?

Interrupting my fickle thoughts, I feel Brian's warm palm

rest on my back.

"I'm proud of you, Mark," he starts, and I turn, surprised to find glassy pools resting in the corner of his eyes. "Seeing the man you've become—watching you grow into the alpha I've always known you to be. I'm so frigging proud of you!" Pulling me into a hard bear hug, Brian squeezes me tight. "Now go clean yourself up, so we can kick these Primes out of our parish!" He whispers in my ear, adding a hearty laugh to cover his words, before slapping my back hard once more.

The one time I actually need Brian's pessimism, here he is being supportive.

Thanks a lot, B.

Turning his attention back to us, Jackson claps his hands hard. "Ahh, now that's what I like to see. Camaraderie."

Brian remains at my side, his chest puffed with pride. And while the thought of washing Braelyn off me, pains me more than any of them can understand, I work hard to shrug my dismay. I know this is for the best.

"For now, young alpha, you tend to yourself. I trust your second can gather your things to be sent to the old den keep for the rituals. Dranoel just informed me he's tasked his apprentice, Lorien with assisting in gathering the women for the processional. I'll go over everything with you when you arrive. You'll only have about a half hour to prepare yourself. The sun is setting soon, and we'll need to safely get you and your mate to the keep before too many of those rabid creatures make their run through the city."

Jackson's eyes stay pinned on me after he speaks. I can only wonder if he's waiting for me to run and forget this nonsense. A part of me feels like he wouldn't condemn me if I did. Goodness knows Brian hardly wants me to do this, but with the new pride I see puffing through his chest, I hate to disappoint him so soon. Even more, I know I can't let the pack down. No doubt there's a stirring of restlessness since I lost my betrothed, Braelyn, only weeks ago.

Truthfully, we had only a brief, albeit blissful, four weeks together before our world came crashing down. Sure, I may have pined over her not long after my first teen crush kicked me to the curb, but who would blame me? Braelyn was one of the coolest, most down to earth vampires I ever met. Although she spent years never giving me a second thought, when our moment came, I went after her with everything I had. And she let me.

But I'm no idiot. Braelyn had her heart broken plenty of times before me. I mean everyone knows she had her heart set on that Altrinion Vampire Titan for most of her vampire existence. Instead of treating her like the rare ruby she was, he couldn't commit. Or wouldn't. Who knows?

His loss was certainly my gain.

Even if that gain was for such a short time.

So here I am, wearing the remains of the one person I thought I was supposed to spend the rest of my life with. Yet knowing with the look my Prime Alpha is giving me, it's time for me to wash away the remnants of the one whose smile alone brightened my life more than I thought a wretch like me deserved.

Now I know the truth. I don't deserve true love. Hell, I probably shouldn't even be here. But I am. And since I am, I'll do what I was put on this earth for. Protect and serve. If that means choosing a mate I do not love, so be it.

"Yes, my lord," I answer, squaring my shoulders and lifting my chin from my chest. "I'll prepare myself as is required. Let the copula ritual commence."

Chapter 5

"What if this doesn't work, Braelyn? I would never forgive myself if something happened to you because of me." I groan into our kiss, cupping the nape of her neck in my palm.

"Oh shush! When you follow your heart, things have a way of working out the way they should," Brae smiles back, puckering a kiss on my nose. "Besides even if it didn't work, it would all be worth it for me."

"How could you say that baby?"

"I never thought anyone could look at me the way you are right now. I might be human now, but only a few hours ago, I was a cold-veined leech. You fell for a Scourge vampire, remember? But when you look at me, you see me. Not some vile creature. If I had to die right now, I'd die happy. Happy, because I was loved by you."

Memories of one of the last times I held Brae in my arms flash through my mind as I stand in the shower. Had I known the next morning all I'd have left were her ashen remains, I would have held her tighter.

I would have made love to her.

But we wanted to wait.

You know, do it right.

Imprinting is a tricky thing between wolves and others.

Even tricker for virgins like me. If for any reason my wolf didn't accept Braelyn as my mate, just the intercourse alone could prove deadly.

I thought if we were mated through the covenant of marriage, it would ensure the mating took. Instead, we never made it down the aisle and I lost her anyway.

Keeping my eyes fixed on the drain as thick, chalky, gray dust settles around my feet I watch as her remains disappear down the dark abyss. Stinging tears mixed with heavily chlorinated water pour down my face as I press my palms into the tile wall while standing beneath the shower spray.

Shit.

This hurts.

And it hurts bad.

Banging my fist against the wall, a loud roar erupts from me, and I know my pain can likely be heard throughout the tavern. A small crack ripples between the grout lines and marble tile and I shout again.

This is all my fault. Not the stupid crack—but all of this.

Braelyn is dead because of me.

The Dunes pack may fall to ruin because of me.

Everyone who has ever cared anything about me has either died or is on the edge of death itself.

First there was Dauphine. I may not have liked her as much as I did her best friend, and my first teen love, Claudia, but I did care for her. But now she's dead. The day I told her I wasn't interested in her—because I wanted to be with Braelyn—she was later killed by Scourge vampires.

Then there is Jerrica. Sure there was never anything romantic between us, but she was my friend. She still is. And a mentor to both me and Brian. Even though everyone thinks she's just a snooty Altrinion vampire, she's only ever shown me kindness. But now she lays at the brink of death all at the hands of Claudia.

And even Claudia, my first teen love, and the first person to ever break my heart, is now on the run. All because she stabbed Jerrica. I can hardly believe she's the same girl I played spin the bottle with and shared my first kiss. What she'd have to gain by hurting Jerrica I'll never understand. But she will pay for her crimes.

But my beloved Braelyn didn't deserve this.

I only have myself to blame.

"I'm sorry Brae," I cry against the stream of water running down my face. "I promise I won't let them forget you. Your name will live on. In me. *I promise.*"

With my eyes shut tight, I trail my palm up the seam of the wall and find the shower hose. Pulling it from its holster, I spray around my feet. Heaving hard air as I do, I open my eyes and watch Braelyn's ashes pool around my feet before descending down the drain.

I've buried both of my parents, but this is, by far, the hardest thing I've ever done.

The last grain glides past me and I drop the hose to my side, exhaling the curdling breath within me.

Damn. She's gone.

I can feel it now.

As much as I want for nothing than to wrench my finger down the drain and pull whatever is left of her back up, I cannot.

Braelyn would want me to move on.

She would want me to remember my duty to my pack.

Braelyn gave her life so that I could protect my pack. She

gave up her vampirism in an attempt to become human just so I could carry on my bloodline and ensure the safety of my pack. I'll not let her death be in vain. Not now or ever.

Placing the hose back into the holster, I quickly lather the sponge with soap and scrub away. Although, I'm doing this to make myself presentable and ensure my weeks' worth of funk doesn't screw up the mating rites, I know Braelyn would want me looking my best.

She always said I cleaned up good for a mutt.

Just the thought of her poking fun at me over the years, makes me laugh. For the first time, a real genuine laugh. And it's all because of her.

As I continue washing, I can't help recounting all the times she made fun of me. In fact, she made fun of everyone. Braelyn always said people took themselves way more seriously than they should. I liked that about her. Despite living through some of the most tumultuous times in her two hundred and thirty years, she always found a way to be a bright light in our very dark world.

I loved that about her.

In a weird way, I feel like if she could tell me anything from the great beyond, she'd tell me things have a way of working out the way they should. She'd tell me to go through this mating ritual with an open mind.

Even though Brae would despise the thought of a man choosing a woman at a whim, she'd tell me to be better than my father.

Live honorably.

Above all, Brae would tell me to follow my heart.

And that is exactly what I plan to do.

Chapter 6

"Looking like a pure-bred alpha!" Jackson merrily announces with his arms outstretched to greet me as I make my way down the narrow corridor.

Brian grumbles something behind me in response, but I choose to ignore him. It took enough to get me out of my suite in the first place. I don't have the energy for whatever negative vibe he's giving toward Jackson.

Instead, I take a moment to appreciate the almost handsome guy staring back at me in the mirror. Although I didn't take time to shave, I'm slightly digging this ruggish new look. The full beard looks better on me than I thought. And while I've been known for my perfect gel-to-mousse ratio, my natural wavy brunette hair plays against the contrast of the bluish-green eyes I inherited from my mother, and it makes me smile.

Still, I'm surprised Jackson isn't offput by my denim and black tee. With him and the other prime wolves donned in suits, I certainly look like the odd man out.

I've always heard the primes were a dapper and debonair bunch, but Jackson and his den look like they just stepped out of an *Esquire* photo shoot. But you couldn't tell by how my Prime Alpha greets me. It's as though I'm wearing a three-piece suit, by the way he's staring at me.

Pulling me in for an embrace, Jackson smiles. "You are certainly one of Louisiana's finest!"

"Thank you, my lord," I reply, patting his back.

Squeezing my shoulder, Jackson's eyes narrow into mine as he searches my face. "Listen, Mark, I know this is not the way you wanted to mate, but just trust the process. Trust your wolf. He will not guide you astray."

At his words, I work hard to choke back my tears. I haven't shifted in weeks. My wolf pounded within me to be set free at Braelyn's passing, but I refused him. Since then he's been silent. If I didn't know it was impossible, I could almost believe my wolf abandoned me. That's just how quiet he's been.

How can I expect my wolf to guide me in this process when I've barely interacted with him?

"What is it?" Jackson asks, pulling my arm and walking me to a corner away from Brian and some of the other primes gathered near the stairwell. "Please, Mark, you can tell me."

I guess the look on my face is obvious. Either that or Brae was right. I don't have a poker face.

I take a quick peek over Jackson's shoulder, and I see Brian talking with Dilano and Cal. Brian nods at me with a small smile before brushing his dirty blonde hair behind his ear, faking interest in whatever Cal is sharing.

"Mark?" Jackson calls my attention back to him.

Biting my lip, I look around and see Bessie talking with another woman at the end of the hall and my stomach knots, knowing she's likely finalizing everything to bring in the prospects.

I can't believe I'm really doing this.

Firming his hold on my shoulder, Jackson shifts so that he is once more in my eyesight.

"I'm sorry, my lord, it's nothing. Really."

Jackson's mouth crests into a thin line and he grunts. He's not buying it.

"Well, it's just what if my wolf doesn't guide me to anyone? I mean, I haven't shifted in weeks. Besides, I think he's pretty pissed at me."

Relaxing his grip, Jackson laughs, stepping back slightly. "Oh, I wouldn't worry about that." Covering his laugh, his eyes glance around the hallway for a minute before he turns us, so our backs are to everyone. "With all the peony, orchid, and rose scents Sophie and Bessie have smelling about the tavern, I'm sure your wolf will be more concerned about mating than anything. Even if he were mad at you, his instinct to mate is stronger than any petty differences you two may share."

Gulping, I realize what Jackson is talking about.

Sex.

It's a copula ritual, idiot. What did you think you were coming here for?

Great, now my wolf is mocking me. This horny SOB has been plotting against me the entire time.

A small rumble moves through my chest and my nose flares as I take in the fragrant scents musing about the tavern. My posture straightens and for the first time in a while, I feel my wolf move inside me.

Horny bastard.

"I guess you're right," I smile back. Then I remember and my face goes red.

"What's wrong, Mark?" Jackson whispers, concern filling between his brows.

"How does this work exactly? I mean—um—if you've never—"

Jackson's eyes grow wide with surprise, and I see his cheeks blush behind his goatee. With his hand once more covering his mouth he leans into me. "You're a virgin?"

Looking around the hall, I'm thankful to see everyone, including Brian, enthralled in their own conversations. Good.

I nod in reply only and Jackson exhales, locking our arms tight.

"Trust your wolf." Burrowing his gaze into mine, it's as though he was talking more to my wolf than me. "You're going to smell pheromones at their highest peak. That's why Sophie's dressed the place with all manner of floral and garden scents to ensure the most natural of responses. As you pass by the potentials, your wolf will lock in on the scent that captures him. The scent that makes him stand still and all the world go silent. It will whip about you in such an intense manner, you'll want for nothing than to stop everything and claim her as your mate."

Looking at the distant gaze now set in Jackson's eyes, it's clear that while he's talking to me, he's thinking about her. Damina. His one true love.

Damn, I know this must be hard for him.

Because it certainly is for me.

"Yes, my lord," I softly answer. This time it's me, shifting myself so that I recapture his attention.

Rocking back on his heel, he shakes his head, forcing his thoughts of his beloved aside. "Like I said, young alpha, trust your wolf." He smiles again, and this time it reaches his eyes. "Don't worry about being experienced or not. Mating is a natural experience. Let your heart and your wolf lead the way and you'll be just fine."

My heart?

Trust my wolf? Fine.

Trust my heart? Jury is still out.

"But what if—"

Before I can get out my protest, the sound of a loud chime from the end of the hall silences us all.

"It's time!" Bessie announces from the top of the main staircase.

Jackson turns his attention back to me as he lifts his fingers in the air, snapping for Gregory to come to his side. "I'll see you soon. Like I said, everything will be fine." Patting my back hard, Jackson quickly makes his way down the hall with Gregory on his heel.

Many of the other wolves follow them as Brian and Cal make their way toward me. I'm not really sure what to do, but I figure I should stay put. If Jackson wanted me to follow him, he would've told me.

"They'll send someone for you shortly," Cal says as he saunters to my corner of the hallway with his hands stuffed in his pockets. With a chewing stick swirling the corner of his mouth, he leans against the wall and sighs as his fedora falls to his forehead, resting on his nose. His dark brown skin seems to glow beneath the warm sconce lights in the hall. I watch as his chest heaves, expanding and retracting as though he were resisting a shift.

Looking over my shoulder at Brian, I notice even he has a slight glow about him. Wolves are prone to glisten a bit before a shift, but this seems different. What's strange is that as I gaze around, all the remaining wolves in the hall seem to be just as affected as both Brian and Cal.

Everyone except me.

"B," I whisper, tugging his arm. A low rumble pulls through

him as he turns to me, and I see his eyes flash gold. I step back, wondering if his wolf is about to take over. "What's going on?" I ask.

Brian only grumbles in return, breathing heavy and working hard to keep his wolf at bay.

"It's the mating call," Cal answers, tipping his forefinger to his brim so that I can now see his sun-spun eyes glowing back at me. He lets out a breath and pulls himself from the wall as he rests his hat back to his head. "Lord Nashoba has officially begun the call of the copula ritual. The incense and florals you smell also work as an aphrodisiac. Wolves who are already mated feel the pull stronger than most. Everything inside us right now is telling us to find our partners and mate."

I gulp.

Crap. So basically, I'm standing around a bunch of lust-fueled wolves.

"Yeah, so the faster you pick a mate, the better for us all." Cal laughs, loosening the collar on his shirt.

Brian laughs with him, and I try to shrug off how uncomfortable I feel. Looking around I even notice Dilano and his lady Alana, leaned into one another in front of a door I'm sure they're supposed to be guarding.

Only two seem just as uncomfortable as me. Gregory and Lorien. Lorien, I get since he's barely nineteen. But Gregory surprises me. For as cocky as the overgrown lug is, I was sure someone like him has already mated.

Then I remember, he had his eyes on Dacari.

I can't help wondering what I have missed all the days I was held up in my room.

But I know one thing, from the way Brian is reacting, it's clear he's mated.

Slapping his shoulder hard, I smile. "Really, B? You weren't going to tell me you mated Dacari?"

Pulling my arm, Brian leans into me, nostrils flared and breathing hard. "Hey, Mark, keep it down! We're still working things out, you know?" His widened, dancing, eyes alone tell me he's literally over-the-moon in love, but he wants discretion. I get it, but I can't help being happy for him.

"Promise me we'll talk?" I try to sound serious, but I'm bubbling over inside knowing the one guy I think of like a brother finally has found happiness. Even if it's with the daughter of the devil.

But that's another story. And the real reason why these rabid creatures are running amuck.

"Hey, did you tell him about Claudia?" Cal jabs Brian in the side and I know it's his way of changing the conversation.

Brian's posture relaxes a bit, but he tenses some as he turns back to me. I'm sure the thought of what Claudia did to Jerrica strikes a nerve capable of even dousing the mating call.

"Claudia? What about her?" I'm curious. Last I heard she was on the run after she stabbed Jerrica.

"We caught her." The lilt in Brian's tone gives off a sigh of relief. "Yep, some of the Guard caught her trying to sneak back into the mansion. I guess she was trying to finish what she started."

While it's hard for me to believe this is the same girl I used to love, I'm glad they caught her. She needs to pay for what she did to Jerrica.

"That's good to hear, Brian. Perhaps now we can—"

A loud throat clearing from a tall man standing at the front of room with Jackson, interrupts us.

"Lord Helsing," Jackson says in a more commanding tone.

"Come forward."

My feet quickly adhere to my Prime Alpha's command, and I can almost feel my wolf pulling me along.

Trust my wolf. I recant to myself. It's about time I let him lead the way.

Chapter 7

Walking down the long corridor toward Jackson, I am overwhelmed at the crescent bow each wolf gives as I pass by. While it may be a normal gesture to offer a formal curtsy in the presence of an alpha, it's still a strange feeling knowing that alpha is me.

I barely had time to absorb becoming the lead alpha of Louisiana and reinstating the Beta Primes before my world went to hell at Braelyn's passing. No sooner than I became alpha did my life fall apart. I've given one, maybe two commands as alpha, yet I have folk bowing to me now.

This is going to take some getting used to.

Extending his hand toward me, Jackson gestures for me to come to his side. Gregory takes a few steps behind Jackson, leaving us at the center of the room.

Lifting his hand with his fist tightened, every wolf pounds their own chest, lowering their heads in submission.

"You may be seated," Jackson directs the pack.

For a minute, I wonder if there are enough seats for everyone. But when they scurry into the darkness where I now see folding chairs placed along the wall, I realize who the small array of seats is for in the middle of the room.

This is really about to happen.

"We are all gathered this evening to bear witness to our sacred ritual of copula. As such, and to ensure the alpha bloodline, Lord Mark Avram Helsing will invoke his right to mate. Of you here, are there any sufficient to challenge his invocation?"

"Not I." A chorus of golden eyes flash along the shadowed wall as each den leader affirms my right to mate.

Turning to me, Jackson offers a small smile before looking over his shoulder and nodding to Sophie. Quickly snapping her fingers to Lorien and Dranoel, they open two large walnut doors where Bessie now stands in front of a line of potential mates.

Slowly pacing into the center of the room, Jackson looks around so that his eye meets every den leader assembled. "Then so be it. Without objection, each of you solemnly swears to accept and submit to the coupling. Let the copula commence!"

Waving his hand to Sophie, she steps in front of Bessie as they lead the processional of potentials.

Adorned in dark hooded cloaks, with their heads low, I see no identifying parts of any of the women, save their height. Jackson wasn't lying when he said I had to trust my wolf. There's no way I'll see their eye color, smile or even their figure. This is mating in its purest sense.

The processional is led before the den leaders first, then they are assembled in rows of four in the center of the room.

"You may be seated," Jackson says in a milder tone than earlier. Turning to me, he extends his hand, motioning for me to begin.

Although I am uncertain on how this will play out, there's an instinctual force guiding my steps.

Taking a deep breath as I make my way toward the potentials, I inhale the fragrant scents and I feel my muscles tighten beneath my skin. Flexing and contorting as though I were about to shift, a low growl rumbles through me. My nose flares and I detect the varying scents coming from each candidate.

Some are inviting and some repugnant.

Like flowers and filth.

Stepping in front of my first one, her scent is sweet, but almost too much. It makes my stomach hurt, like I ate a bag full of candy. Letting out a loud yelping howl, I see the woman tremble beneath me as I tower over her. In that moment, Sophie snaps her fingers and the same man from before quickly comes to take the woman away.

The next woman's scent reeks. So much so, I want to vomit. This time my howl is more aggressive than before. Sophie doesn't even bother to snap her fingers this time, as the man is at her side in an instant, removing the woman.

Circling the huddle of remaining potentials, I'm thankful their scents aren't as nauseating as the first two. My wolf propels my motion around the women like a funnel. In an almost stalking manner, I lean into the candidates, inhaling copious amounts of their scents. Working hard to distinguish one aroma from the next, I linger a bit in front of each candidate. Smells of rose, sandalwood, and something strangely inviting I cannot place petal past my nose.

But I want to know it.

I want to savor it.

Devour it.

Turning a bit so that I get a breath of fresh air, I step away from the women. But I cannot stay away for long. The unknown scent is luring me back in. No sooner than I can blink, I find myself back in the huddle.

Crouching low, I circle the women once more. Heaving in large gulps of their array of fragrance, I quickly howl over two others, and they are pulled from the group. Only eight remain and it's getting harder to place their scents, as a new aroma, fear, now permeates through their pores.

I can't see which are wolves, Altrinion, or human, but I know my boorish outbursts and growls are becoming too much. The last thing I need is the smell of fear infiltrating the purity of their scents.

Working hard to pace my breathing, I croon a low hum. Baying to settle a pack is a talent only inherent in alphas. It's a talent I've never used before, but this feels like the most appropriate thing to do to slow the already erratic heartbeats of the potentials.

As I do, I hear the pacing of their collective hearts settle. Good.

But this time their pheromones smell different. All except for one, that is. While the seven remaining aromas still retain their flowery essence, only one stands out just like before.

Yet, this time the scent is stronger. So strong in fact, it draws me close.

Pulling me, no yanking me, almost violently, into the center of the eight remaining women. Four of the women fall from their seats, scampering to get away from me. Three start to cry, holding tight to one another, likely fearful of what I'll do next.

Licking my lips, I notice my canines have lengthened. Looking at my hands, I see my claws pointed and thick fur resting along my forearm.

In the tussle of it all, I hadn't realized my repose was in

mid-shift.

I suppose it explains their fear.

Still one remains unmoved.

Almost defiant.

Willful.

And I like it.

The other women are quickly removed from the huddle leaving me alone with the one scent that has me in a literal tailspin.

My heart thumps violently in my chest and I let out a surging howl. But she does not move. She remains in her seat. Covered fully in her hooded cloak, I wish I could see her eyes. I need to see this elusive one who refuses to quake at my call. What color, I wonder, will her eyes be when she looks defiantly into my own?

Do her lips curve as she sets her will to match mine?

I need to know. And I want to know now.

Once more, her fragrance sends stirrings inside me I'd not known I was capable of until now. Even the strength of my manhood jumps at the tantalizing call of her pheromones mixing harmoniously with mine.

My knees buckle, and I want for nothing than to pull this woman to my side and nestle her in my arms. Hovering the crown of her head, I take in another whiff and just her scent sends me to my knees. Bowed before her, tremors of an ecstasy I've never known pour over me.

Instinct leads me to her feet, and I work my way up her legs, sniffing her from her calves to her knees. There's a familiarity to her that is both comforting and curious.

Who is this woman?

Trust my wolf. I hear my Prime Alpha's words echoed in my

memory. So I let him lead. And lead me he does. Trailing my nose further to her thighs, the sweet smells exuding from her femininity strike a chord in me I once swore only belonged to Braelyn.

It almost feels wrong. Almost. But my wolf refuses to let the thought linger.

Instead, he drives me just shy of her sweet spot forcing me to draw in the intoxicating scent of her. She is a whole muse! A chorus of melodies implode my mind at the call of her scent. It's taking every bit of my restraint not to claim her right here in front of all.

Low, sensual groans echo throughout the room. Now the heady atmosphere from before makes sense to me.

I feel it too.

The copula.

Panting, I sit back on my knees and let out one final shrieking yelp. Claps and cheers erupt around us, and I finally feel at ease. Slowly, my canines retract and my fur fades as my heart rate settles.

I haven't even seen her face, but I know with all confidence I have indeed chosen my mate.

If someone would have told me when I awoke today, this would be my lot, I wouldn't believe them. Now, here I sit at the feet of one mated to be my equal and I am speechless.

"Well, it appears Lord Helsing has chosen his mate!" Jackson says to a cheerful audience. Once more, the sound of cheers and clapping reverberates throughout the room as Jackson makes his way to my side. Placing his hand on my shoulder, he looks around the room, waving his hand to settle the onlookers. "Lord Helsing," he begins regaining my attention. "Do you swear by the rites of copula to accept your mate as your equal?"

My heart smiles. And for the first time in a while, I feel something I hadn't expected to find. Happiness.

As though a big weight were removed from my chest, I let out an exasperated "Yes."

Affirming praise booms around the room, and I smile, laughing with a new sense of glee I haven't felt in far too long.

Extending his hand to help me from the floor, Jackson pulls me into a quick embrace. Squeezing my shoulder tight, he smiles proudly back at me before turning me to face the candidate.

"Would you like to meet your mate, Lord Helsing?" He announces merrily.

My heart races a bit and sweat forms at my brow. I'm nervous. But I'm also excited. I feel like a kid at Christmas. I nod in affirmation and Jackson gestures his palm for me to do the honors.

Taking a deep breath, I close my eyes and carefully place my hands on her hood.

This morning I had no idea I could feel like this. Giddy. Excited. I can only hope the fates don't let me down again. Perhaps this time happiness won't evade me as quickly as it came.

Chapter 8

Trembling, my fingers twine between the hem of the hood of her cloak, slowly pulling it down. I feel my heart pounce as I watch my newly pronounced mate's luscious, wavy, and thick, ginger-laced tresses fall free.

As my eyes linger at the way her hair drapes along her shoulders the pacing of my heart quickens. But the thumping I feel is not one of lust nor of the well-spring of passion budding in me only moments ago.

Rather, the thumping I now feel is one of shock, awe, and a dreadful sense of familiarity. These aren't the tresses of some stranger hand-picked by Sophie for the copula. The strands softly laying on the shoulders in front of me now are ones I've seen and touched before.

It couldn't be.

No.

"Behold, your alpha. Behold your mate!" Jackson proudly pronounces as more tremors shoot up my spine.

Squeezing my eyes tight, I shake my head, worried of who I'll see looking back at me.

"Lord Helsing!" Jackson commands me, with a swift pat to my back.

I flinch as soon as he does and I grunt, knowing full well

who I'll find when I open my eyes.

"No!" I hear Brian growl behind me just as I force my eyes open.

More gasps echo throughout the hall, but it's too late.

The gnawing angst within me is proven correct.

Looking up at me with wide eyes and a tightened half-smile is Claudia DeVeaux. The wretched, descendent of the villainous Chartreuse Grenoble, Claudia DeVeaux. How the woman who stabbed my mentor and friend Jerrica and was once my first love is seated before me, I'll never understand.

But I know one thing.

The Fates or the Powers-that-Be are some sadistic bastards who don't give two nuts about me. Or perhaps this is someone's idea of a sick twisted joke.

Yet, with the way my Prime Alpha is looking at me now, it's clear even he is mortified at my supposed match.

"This can't be, my lord," I huff over my shoulder. "Did I do something wrong?"

Taking my forearm in his grip, his eyes grow wide at my admission, and he too, steps back, speechless.

"How the hell did she get in the line up?" Brian shouts, making his way to my side. Leaning over Claudia, Brian lets out a loud growl and his nostrils flare as he stares down at her.

Strangely, my instincts pull me from Jackson's hold, and I place myself in front of Claudia, blocking Brian. Still, his chest continues heaving hard while a stirring of disbelief grows around us.

"Brian, step back!" I grit my words, almost hating myself for defending her. But I can't help it.

Brian is furious and he has every right to be. He's pledged his loyalty to cover Jerrica, as a wolfen guardian to an Altrinion, the most sacred of supernaturals. By rights, it's a wolf's duty to pledge our protection to Altrinions in general, but as a sacred guardian, such protection is akin to the covenant of marriage, without the consummate intimacy.

Even as Jackson stares between us, he understands Brian's rage. As Jackson has pledged such a protection to Damina. She's not only his mate, but one he's been given charge to protect.

More growls and snarls echo throughout the room and the new fear I feel is not one of mere dread, but a looming fear for the one who was just pronounced my mate. And with the glowing eyes shimmering throughout, I feel the threats of their searing gaze boiling in my blood.

But we won't let them touch her.

What the fu—

I don't have time to ponder my inner conflict with my wolf, when I hear Jackson force a throat clearing, lifting his fist to calm the outrage simmering about the tavern.

"Young woman," Jackson begins, turning sharply on his heel toward Claudia, "please stand."

Claudia quickly does as she's instructed, but not before freeing herself from the heavy cloak, dropping it onto the chair behind her. I can't help marvel at her defiant stance as she squares her shoulders, folding her arms behind her, clasping her wrists.

With glistening pouty lips and a black tank, showcasing her perfect abs and full rack, she keeps her eyes forward, not facing any of us. And while she looks like the girl I've known since I learned my own name, there seems to be something different about her.

Sure, most knew her to be the daughter of the human leader

of the faction of nobles, but I knew her as the first girl my lips touched. For a good portion of my life, we were inseparable. So when we played spin the bottle and landed our first lip-lock, I always thought she would be my person. My everything.

That is, until she set her sights higher than a raggedy Dunes wolf like me. From the time we were eighteen until what seems like only yesterday, she'd done everything possible to gain the favor of Lord Dalcour Marchand. Not only is he the leader of the vampire faction, but being Altrinion, was of a higher class than a subservient like me.

But I can't say I dawdled on her heels. No sooner than she set her attention elsewhere, did my father teach me the "lay of the land." My gigolo padre made it his first-right to teach me how to work the room and master my charm. While I never rose to the occasion in his eyes by bedding anything with a skirt before he died, he at least approved that I may indeed be a chip off the old block.

I can thankfully say I am anything but.

As much as I'd like to believe that Claudia has perhaps changed for the better, I know the truth. She sought to kill Jerrica.

Stepping in front of me and breaking my musing, Jackson's eyes lock with mine. "Lord Helsing," Jackson begins while shooting a sharp gaze toward Claudia. "Does her scent still catch you?"

I don't even have to inhale a heap of air to know the truth.

The answer is a most resolute *yes.*

In fact, I'm buzzing inside with an intensity I've never known until now.

The magnetism of Claudia DeVeaux pulls me like a moth to a flame. And yet even the fear of being burned by her does little to douse the kindling flame building inside me at the call of her scent.

Sweat thickens along my brow and my breathing quickens. I even fear I'll shift right here. With the way my wolf is raging to be set free and claim her here and now, it's taking all of my might to remain poised before my Prime Alpha and this den of onlookers.

Just as I part my lips to reply, Jackson softly places his hand on my shoulder, narrowing his eyes and sighing a little as he regards me. "I think I have my answer," he says, tilting his eyes downward. Following his gaze, I quickly bring my hands in front of my crotch, hopeful to cover the stiffening, throbbing member in my jeans.

Great. Now I have two monsters inside me fighting for their release.

"Lord Nashoba," Brian begins, his tone brusque, "this woman has betrayed her status of nobility. She has attempted to kill an Altrinion. And it is our duty to protect the Order of Altrinion above all."

I don't have a chance to rebuke Brian before Jackson quickly leans into him, growling with his eyes glowing bright. "Brian! Mind your place! Do not speak to me of duty, young wolf! I, above all assembled here tonight keep a manner of propriety a second-rate moon walker such as yourself could not fathom! Let this be the last time you test the measure of my resolve. I swear the next time you do, you will surely meet your end!"

Lowering his eyes, Brian's lips tighten, and I can tell it's taking everything within him keeping him steady.

"Sophie!" Jackson calls to his aunt over his shoulder without taking his eyes off Brian.

Taking careful steps toward us and with Bessie at her side,

Sophie keeps her eyes lowered as she approaches. "Yes, my lord," she answers with no more than a whisper.

"Was this woman not captured?"

"Yes, my lord."

Grunting, Jackson shifts his attention toward Sophie and Bessie. Both women keep their heads down, but I watch Sophie flit her eyes over her shoulder toward Bessie in blame.

"Well, maybe you can explain how she made it from the detaining cell to the copula ritual. Please tell me we are not so unrefined we can't tell prisoners apart from participants!" Slamming his hands to his sides, I can see his patience with us all has waned.

Pacing back and forth, he looks Bessie and Sophie over, awaiting a response. Instead of a reply, both women shift their posture, one to another.

"If someone doesn't explain something soon I will—"

A small faux cough breaks through Jackson's hard rebuke from behind. Turning our attention toward the door, Cal's lanky cousin, Lorien, makes his way to the center of the floor. "I'm sorry Lord Nashoba," he begins, "the offense rests with me. It seems I made a mistake in which women I was supposed to get."

Jackson laughs. But this laugh carries no merriment. Running his hands through his wavy mane, he circles the floor. "Oh well then it was a mistake! I suppose that makes it all better!" His willfully dark sarcasm is threatening. Our Prime Alpha is pissed.

"No, my lord," I hear both Cal and Dranoel say in unison as they make their way to the center floor where we stand.

"Does anyone not understand the jeopardy you've placed us all in?" Jackson sighs, cupping his hands to his chin as he continues his pacing.

"Please, Lord Nashoba, it was not the boy's mistake entirely," Dranoel starts, with his hands lifted in caution. "We picked up a host of women from our shelter to be participants. The women were only held in our detention area for a short while. When we sent Lorien to get the participants that Sophie prepared, I don't think we were clear with our instructions. The fault, my lord, is not his own."

Stepping in front of Dranoel, Bessie offers a half-witted smile. "My lord, I am the proprietor of this tavern and I take full responsibility for the mistake. Please do not condemn Lorien."

"As do I," Sophie inserts herself to Bessie's side. "I was charged to prepare the women, but I did not see to their final preparations as I should. Had I done so, I would have discovered these women were not those among our earlier selection."

Dragging his eyes from Lorien, Sophie, Dranoel and Bessie, Jackson carries his darted glare across the room. "So what happened to those of your choosing?"

Lorien steps forward. "We believe they are still in the holding center, my lord. It's no trouble, I can simply go get them and—"

"That won't be necessary!" Jackson barks back over his shoulder.

For a moment I feel a modicum of relief. Perhaps I won't have to tether myself to Claudia after all.

"The copula has been accepted. It cannot be reverted." Jackson says, making his way to the doors at the main hall.

"But my lord," Brian pleads, coming to my side. "If these women weren't in the selection, then how can the copula be deemed official?"

A chorus of questions rings through the hall, and I know most think the same.

"It is official. It's done. Once Lord Helsing took in her scent and laid claim, his pronouncement was assured. There is no going back."

"Lord Nashoba," I begin, stepping only slightly from Claudia's side. With the low growls Brian is issuing, I still don't trust he won't snap.

Exasperated, Jackson turns back to face me. Gone are the cheerful curves of his smile or glimmer in his eyes. If I didn't know better, I'd think Jackson would rather walk away from this chaos and let the rabid monsters taking over our city have their way. Extending his hand toward me, he gestures for me to speak.

"Brian is right, my lord. If Claudia tried to kill an Altrinion, there's no way I can pronounce her as my mate. Right?"

Slowly, Jackson paces toward me. Letting out a heavy sigh, he grumbles something before looking back at me. "If only, Lord Helsing, it was that easy. But it's not. The pronouncement has been made."

Keeping his gaze set on Claudia, Brian's chest rumbles some. "I thought our duty to protect Altrinions was above all."

"No Brian," Dranoel chimes in from across the room. "I'm afraid Lord Nashoba is correct. While our duty to the Order of Altrinion is indeed high, nothing takes precedence over a pack's need for procreation."

"Dranoel speaks the truth," Jackson adds, sauntering back into the center of the room. "There are few things keeping any of us from turning into the one thing we all fear. Skull wolves. Monstrous beasts who've broken the bonds of kinship and mating. Packless. Leaderless. Even prime wolves must not be found in dereliction. With exception to hybrid wolves, any wolf found as such will face a fate of a Skull. It is for this reason, Young Alpha, that the pronouncement of your mate bears weight. And with your oath to the Order of Altrinion when they removed the Dunes curse from your pack, you sealed your own fate. Therefore, Lord Helsing, the mating has officially commenced."

A stinging ache shoots through me, knowing I am bound to Claudia DeVeaux is a pain that seems almost unbearable. As if losing Braelyn wasn't hard enough, now I'm stuck with someone who has not only broken my heart but tried to kill someone I care for.

But still, I have no choice but to proceed with the mating. I've failed my pack once already and I won't be the cause of my den being cursed again or falling to a Skull's lot.

This is the first decision I'll make as an Alpha of the Beta Primes.

There is no going back now.

Chapter 9

"Lord Nashoba," Sophie starts with a light cough, and I am thankful for her interruption. Making her way toward where me and Claudia stand, Sophie casts an awkward smile. Offering an affirming nod, Jackson's eyes soften as he gazes at his aunt. "Perhaps we should ask the young woman if she is amenable. As is our ritual, she does have the option to reject the mating. Of course, as alpha, Lord Helsing, can certainly elect to court her until the mating is complete."

Issuing a loud growl, Brian grunts in response. "We don't have time for this!" Stomping in a circular pace, Brian shoves his hands in his pockets, fuming mad.

Looking behind Sophie, Jackson grimaces as he regards Brian, but I'm surprised when his face also tightens as he sets his attention back to his aunt. "Brian is right, Sophie. We don't have time to commence a courtship."

"Still, Sophie is right, my lord," Dranoel adds. "While we may not have time for a courtship, the mating will not take if the young lady is not agreeable to the idea. If Lord Helsing's wolf senses any apprehension, the mating could be catastrophic. Maybe even deadly for a mortal."

"Well there's the silver lining." Brian snickers.

Quickly, my head rears over my shoulder at Brian as my eyes widen with a scolding stare and he steps back slightly shocked.

Gripes and growls echo throughout the hall as disputes and murmurs ignite among the onlookers. Plunging his head into his palms, Jackson sighs hard, before looking back at me, frustrated. Slowly he lifts his fist to quiet the room.

But before he has a moment to speak, I feel Claudia move at my side for the first time. With her eyes closed, she takes a deep breath, exhales, and opens her eyes again.

"I'll do it." Despite the quietness of her tone, the room goes still.

Turning to her, my mouth hangs open in shock. "What?" I mumble as I stare on at her. She keeps her sights set on Jackson, but I can tell she's working hard not to look at me.

I am surprised. She had an out. *We had an out.* And she didn't take it.

Why?

"Are you certain, young lady?" Jackson asks, taking a few steps closer. "Do you understand what you're agreeing to?"

"Yes, my lord," she answers without hesitation. "I understand the commitment I am making."

"Claudia—" I begin, but Brian's barking growl interrupts us.

Charging toward us, both Cal and Dranoel grab his arms, keeping him back. "This is ridiculous!" He shouts.

"Brian, calm yourself! That's an order!" I roar back. I've grown tired of his bullying stance. While I know it's truly his instinct to protect me and Jerrica, there's a deeper magic brewing within me, refusing to allow him anywhere near my mate. "You heard Lord Nashoba. We don't have time for this! If Claudia agrees to the mating, then so be it. If nothing comes of this but bedding her to ensure the bloodline, I'll see it done. But you will not hurt her. Not now. Not ever. Is that understood?"

Slowly, Brian's head lowers, and I see a small tear drop to his chin. "This isn't about mating. She tried to kill Jerrica! Or does Jerrica no longer matter to you?"

"I did not!" Claudia bites back with her eyes closed and her hands fisted tight at her sides.

"What?" I say, turning my attention back to her.

Lifting her gaze to mine, she searches my face as I do the same. All I find are glassy pools begging for me to dive deep. Everything inside me wants to comfort the pain I sense brewing within her. But I cannot. Not yet.

"Young woman," Jackson begins, making his way to my side. Placing his hand on my shoulder, he squeezes it, keeping his eyes on Claudia. "Are you saying you did not attempt to murder Lady Jeffers?"

Roaring once more, Brian yanks himself free from Cal and Dranoel's hold. "She's lying! We found the knife on her just before she ran away!"

Squaring her shoulders, Claudia inches just ahead of me as she narrows her eyes, facing Brian head on. "I did not try to kill her! Nor did I try to hurt her. Someone else—but not me!"

"Then who?" Brian barks back.

Biting her bottom lip, Claudia turns her head, swiping her chin on her shoulders. It's the same go-to response I've witnessed from her over the years when she's nervous.

"Brian, back down!" Jackson orders with his fist raised in warning. "Now Claudia—"

"Sapphirus stone!" Claudia yells with her eyes closed. Biting her bottom lip, she looks up at me quickly, before casting a careful glance at Jackson. "My lord," she continues, quivering, with her head lowered. "I will tell you everything, provided a sapphirus stone be made available to me."

More gasps splinter in surprise throughout the hall. No one has dared ask for the sacred stone of truth in years. Whether mortal or supernatural, a holder of the stone is bound by truth as it is a revealer of secrets.

Why would Claudia ask for such a stone? Unless...

"Young woman, do you know what you are asking for?" Jackson quickly counters. "This stone is no mere officiant of truth. It also brings certain death to anyone holding it found in untruth."

Once more taking in a deep breath, Claudia breathes hard, and I see her fist tighten at her sides.

"I understand the risks," she whispers in reply.

"Hmph..." Brian grumbles, turning the attention back to him. "She knows the risk because she's the brat of a noble, fluent in our ways. As such, she knows the Louisiana den hasn't been privy to such a stone in decades! Senior Helsing considered the stones dangerous and had them removed long ago. She knows this! This is just a ruse!"

"This is no ruse, my lord," Claudia protests, keeping her sights on me and Jackson. "As I've said before, I'll adhere to the mating. Louisiana is my home. I care about what happens here—even more than some of you. And if the mating secures the bloodline so that Lord Helsing retains his lordship for no other reason than controlling the Scourge and rabid beasts, then I will do my part. Lord Helsing doesn't need to love me for me to do what is right." Pausing, Claudia's eyes glass, but she sucks in a breath and lifts her chin, retaining the stubborn smirk I once sweared I loved. "After the mating is complete and I've done my part in continuing the Helsing bloodline, should Lord Helsing seek to send me away so be it. Or if the stone reveals any untruth in me, I suppose Brian can see to my demise firsthand."

Snarling, Brian casts a calculating grin in return, rubbing his chin.

"Brian will do no such thing!" I huff, turning back to Brian. Looking at the shock in his face, I am surprised to see the reflection of my glowing eyes mirrored in his own. This time I am certain, he heard both my voice and that of my wolf.

Grunting, Brian lowers his head, lifting his eyes only slightly, narrowing his gaze. "Lord Helsing, I'll always stand at your side, but I'll not allow anyone to hurt you—-especially not a second time! But I will do what I must to procure that stone. The minute you return from the ritual—if she makes it past the coupling—that stone will be waiting for her."

The challenging threat laced within Brian's tone concern me, but his tightened scowl softens some, and I know, despite everything, he means me no harm.

"Ah-hem," Jackson groans, sauntering between me and Brian, breaking our forming stand-off. "If this young woman is amenable to proceeding with the ritual, as Sophie suggested was her choice to make, then we needn't dally with any further posturing." Casting his gaze first to Brian, then back at me, it is clear our Prime Alpha is sending a clear message. Back down.

"Yes, my lord," both Brian and I grunt in unison.

With a raised brow and giving us another once-over, Jackson paces to the center of the hall with his hands in his pockets. "Very well then. Get Lord Helsing and his mate in the transport to the Bayou at the Northern Gates immediately. We can no longer delay their coupling."

"The Northern Gates, my lord?" I frown. Last I heard that old den keep was a run-down refuge.

Reclaiming his normal brightened smile, Jackson laughs. "You are an alpha of the Beta Primes now, Lord Helsing. You will begin to see things with new eyes. And new vision. Your dreams will have purpose. And the nightmares of your past, you'll finally put to an end. What once seemed beyond repair, will make itself new again. But only as you submit to the copula and most of all trust your wolf."

Stepping to my side, Claudia drags her gaze through the length of me. While I still find the glint of stubborn defiance in her eyes, I see in her now something else I'd never thought to find.

Hope.

Chapter 10

Standing in front of the Northern Gates, I am overwhelmed.

With the blue haze of the evening sky illuminating the iron rod fence surrounding this historic den keep of legend, and looking to see Claudia DeVeaux, my newly pronounced mate, standing at my side, overwhelmed is the only word to adequately define the mix of feelings floating through me.

A thick foggy mist covers the hovel where I'll be shacked up with Claudia over the next few days, and I can't help but gulp wondering how my prim and snobbish mate is likely regretting her decision to remain at my side. No doubt she wants to break and run, and yet I can't help but be shocked how unphased she seems.

"Lord Helsing," Dranoel begins, patting my shoulder, breaking me from my musing. Turning to look at him over my shoulder, I am thankful to find his kind eyes and generous smile gleaming back at me. "I can only take you this far, you and Lady—"

"Miss—" I growl in correction. She'll only receive the notable as *Lady* if she makes it through this ritual. Through my periphery I see Claudia's jaw clenches, but she keeps her face forward, watchful of the receding fog covering what is to be our shared respite.

Swallowing hard, Dranoel lowers his eyes quickly, offering only a crumpled smile back at me. "Yes, of course, my lord. I also have this for you," he says, shoving a large duffle to my chest. "It contains all you'll need for your stay."

Tugging the bag in my arms, I grimace. I didn't expect it to be heavy. I shudder to think what is inside.

Snapping his fingers, I see two of our newly trained Guardians appear at the entrance of the gate. "Bailey and Baxter—the LaCroix Twins. They will serve your gate for the remainder of your stay. Should you require anything in the interim they will see to it."

With shoulders squared and standing almost as tall as Jackson, their brawny form alone is threatening enough to dissuade any with untoward desires. And while I don't doubt their muscular frame can keep Claudia and I safe, it's the youthfulness of their faces giving me pause.

Despite their shaven heads and full goatee's, I am aware these barely post-pubescent hybrid wolves are just shy their full fur.

How in the hell can they protect me?

Sensing the apprehension marring my face, Dranoel squeezes my shoulder to regain my attention. "Don't worry, my lord. These two gents faired highest in their class. Besides we have a few more of the Guard along the outpost just beyond the Gates. However, Lord Nashoba wanted to ensure we kept the remainder of the Guard close to the Quarter to ward off both the rabid fiends and Scourge vampires running amuck."

Smiling, I pat Dranoel's back. "Of course, I understand."

"Well, if there's nothing else, I'll leave you two to your business. I'll return for you by sunset after the copula is complete or at the latest, on the seventh day."

Leaning into Dranoel, I turn my back, hopeful Claudia doesn't hear. "When the copula is complete? You don't really want me to call you after we—um—" I frown. The thought of me reporting to someone after I have sex sounds creepy. Not to mention invasive.

Dranoel gives me a knowing grin and pats my shoulder. "No worries, my lord. We'll all know one way or another. All in due time." Tipping the brim of his hat, he winks before turning to go back to the SUV.

And with his parting words, Dranoel jumps back in the SUV and is off before I can say a word.

Hitching the duffle across my shoulder, I make my way to the gate as Claudia follows quietly behind me. Nodding briefly to the LaCroix brothers, they both step to either side of the gate.

Standing before iron rails, I see a lock and wonder if Dranoel forgot to give me a key. But before I have a chance to question it further, a strange tightening in my chest rumbles through me. Issuing a loud howl, I am surprised to see the gates open.

Shocked, I chuckle, shaking my head at the wonderment of a new addition to my alpha repertoire.

Trust my wolf.

I hear Jackson's voice echo in my mind, and I think I'm starting to understand there's more to my wolf than I've known.

"Mark, how did you do that?" Claudia exclaims with one hand covering her mouth. Looking up at me, she smiles, and I'm surprised to find her eyes dancing. Maybe there's still a sliver of the girl I used to know hiding beneath the surface.

Who knows? Either way, I know I'm not quite ready to let

my guard down around her. Brian is right. For all I know she's using this opportunity to kill me in my sleep.

Grunting, I shrug my shoulders and continue forward. As I do, I notice Claudia's posture slowly tighten. I'm sure she's not too keen on seeming the least bit interested in me.

Making our way through a galley of overgrown shrubbery, we finally arrive at the den keep. Claudia and I share puzzled glances as we stare at the rundown hovel. With broken windows, and tattered shutters, it looks more like a place that should be condemned than a place for coupling. Yet, looking at the large golden oak door before us, it seems like we stepped into a fairytale.

Glistening golden strands of oak shimmer beyond the night sky and the large leaf-like door handle seems otherworldly.

Looking up and down the length of the door, I don't see anywhere to use a key, so I assume I need to repeat the same gesture from before to open it.

Heaving a gulp of air, I release a loud roar. As I do, the shimmering rays dissipate some and then sparkle again. But—nothing. The door doesn't open. Trailing my eyes along the henge and doorpost, I grip it, wondering if there's some special tactic required to open it.

I don't see anything, so I attempt growling once more. And still nothing.

"Mark—" Claudia begins.

Dropping the duffle to the ground, I walk down the stone pathway. "I should check around the side of the den. Maybe there's another entrance."

"But—"

"You stay right here, I'll be back."

Making my way around the den, all I see is brick and stone,

but not another entrance. While I do notice a few portholes for windows, they're all too small for either me or Claudia to squeeze through.

I don't have the energy for this!

My footsteps are heavy as I make my way back to the front.

"Anything?" Claudia asks. Her bright, hazel-green eyes are full of the same hopefulness I'd seen earlier. A part of me hates that I may be letting her down, while the other part of me hates that I even care.

"Nope. I must be doing something wrong."

Charging forward, I take in a deep breath and tense my stance as I would before I shift. Opening my mouth I prepare to let out another growl, until I feel Claudia grab my wrist. Shooting her a rebuking glare as I feel her palms tighten their hold, she flinches. She's been around wolves long enough to know not to get close to a wolf in such a state. But she doesn't stay frazzled for long.

Keeping her distance, she reaches across me, careful not to touch.

With her hand on the leaf-like knob, she turns it. "Maybe this way is easier," she smiles, using her free hand to cover her chuckle.

"Hmph," I sigh, annoyed with myself.

Crossing the threshold, I knock down a few spiderwebs, and Claudia cringes behind me. Using the cloak from earlier, she holds it over her head, peeping just slightly as she tip toes around the fallen leaves and tree branches laying on the floor.

"I suppose no one comes by to clean this place," Claudia mumbles, fussing with the dusty webs, looming about as she takes off her cloak.

I shake my head and laugh. There's the snooty girl I

remember. No amount of mating is going to help her upper-crust attitude.

Claudia continues her snippy complaining from behind me as I look around. There's a small sink in a closet-sized kitchen with a single gas burner. I also see a small fridge and an open brick oven that seems to double as a fireplace opposite the kitchen. Out of the corner of my eye, I spy a small bathroom, that is strangely complete with a shower, sink, and toilet. It's a tight fit, but I doubt either of us will be in there at the same time.

Outside of a small dusty sofa and rocker, I find only one other area drawing my attention. The bedroom.

There's only one. You have to be kidding me.

"Eek!" Claudia squeals, pulling my attention away from the bedroom. "Spiders!!" she screams, leaning against the sofa, lifting her feet from the floor.

Shaking my head and laughing once more, I grab a small wooden broom I see laying against the wall. Sweeping them out of the door, Claudia winces as the spiders make their way outside.

"You know you're bigger than they are, right?"

Hunching her shoulders, she shivers a bit, still uneasy. "Why didn't you just kill them?"

"So is that your first instinct? To kill?" Looking at Claudia's disheartened glare, I almost regret my words as soon as I say them.

Her expression goes cold as she stares at me. "Well, by not killing them when you had an opportunity, you're just tempting fate. I say, why wait." Narrowing her eyes, her nose crinkles and I remember this is still the person who tried to kill my friend.

While her tone is somewhere between sarcastic and threatening, I know one thing. I'm not in the mood for either. Turning away from her, I lift the duffle to the countertop, pulling out the contents.

Two dozen eggs bubble wrapped in a carton, a bag of mixed fruit, a couple pounds of what I presume are either steaks or chops wrapped in waxed paper, a canister of nuts, and water. Seems basic but doable for our stay. I find a few blankets and small pillows as well. But it's the large cast iron skillet I pull out explaining why the duffle was so heavy.

"Mark," Claudia quietly says, tapping my arm. "I can take those and get the bed cleaned up."

"Are you sure?" I ask, surprised by the gesture. The girl I knew never offered to clean up anything.

Grabbing the folded blankets, she brushes past me, and I feel the same pull toward her from earlier, kindling within me once more.

Softly, the tips of her fingers graze mine as she nestles the sheets against her ample bosom. My eyes can't help homing in on the curvature of hips, and thighs, as my eyes trail to her cleavage. Her gaze is almost innocent, hopeful as she stares at me, and I find myself getting lost in the entirety of her.

I'm not ready for this. Not now.

Scooping the blankets from her hold as she turns toward the bedroom, my forearm grazes her breast and I instantly feel myself hardening. I suppose discovering she's braless as her perky nipples point in my direction beneath her dark tank is fueling the horny wolf raging within me.

But he is going to have to wait.

"I've got it." I snap. I don't know who I'm more irritated with, my lust-fueled wolf, or this luscious woman wearing the face of my first love. It doesn't matter. I am not doing this tonight.

Claudia calls after me as I make my way into the bedroom, but I don't answer. All I need right now is for her to stay far from me. Being near her is sending my wolf into overdrive. And while I know the whole point of this is to mate, I know if we're not in perfect harmony, this could turn disastrous. No matter what she has *or hasn't done*, I couldn't bear the thought of another woman dying on my account.

Just as she reaches the threshold of the bedroom, I turn quickly and toss the heavier blanket to her. Dodging, the blanket hits the floor and Claudia throws her hands up, issuing a sharp curse. But I don't care what kind of SOB she's calling me when I see her bend over to gather the blanket. From the roundness of her ass to the bounce of her breast, I know for sure I am making the right decision.

Breathing heavy, I do my best to choke out the words. "Good night, Claudia." As pained as her expression is when I shut the door, little does she know that was the hardest thing I've ever done.

Chapter 11

"*Are you going to sleep the day away, silly?*" *I hear her lilting chuckle, permeate the air, but I don't see her. "Come on, get up already!"*

Loud chirping sounds of birds harp about, and it's a delightful sound to my ears. Faintly, I hear what sounds like waterfalls from afar, but I assume there must be water running outside my room.

"Okay, handsome, see if you can find me..." her voice trails off into the distance, but her giggling sounds only make me want to take her in my arms.

Springing up from the bed, I'm surprised how much light shines into the bedroom. It's as if the sun found its way inside. But as my eyes slowly crack open, I realize I am not in the bedroom. Instead, the bed is in the middle of a garden.

My hands shift along the soft, velvety sheets beneath me, and I know for sure I must be dreaming. This bed feels like a cloud—not the thin, wrought-spring mattress I recall.

Standing from the bed, I gather the sheets around my waist, slightly surprised at my own nakedness. Looking around, I know I should feel alarmed, but there's a strange sense of peace holding me steady.

"Gotcha!" I hear her laugh once more, and it's the sweetest sound I've ever heard. She tugs her small arms around me from behind

and I get goosebumps just knowing she is near. "Aww, come on handsome, turn around. I've waited so long to see you!"

Quickly turning, nothing but a stream of tears race to my chin as soon as I see her. Braelyn.

"Baby, it's you! I never thought I'd see you again!" I cry, lifting her in my arms and twirling her around.

Taking my face in her hands, she leans against my forehead. "I know my Marky! I've missed you!"

"I don't understand, Brae. How is this possible? I—I mean—wait—Claudia! She did it! Brian was right! She slit my throat—smothered me—what!"

"Marky, please calm down, silly!" Brae laughs, kissing my cheek. I want more than a peck on the cheek, but that will have to wait. "Oh, my sweetheart—so full of suspicion. You've been around that bear Brian too long!"

"Brian? What does he have to do with anything? If I'm dead, he has nothing to do with it."

"Baby, you're not dead. This is just a dream. Well, not any dream, but one nonetheless."

Looking at her, I can't help noticing how her skin is almost iridescent, yet pale like a ghost. "I don't understand."

"What have I always told you about Brian? I know he's your best friend, but the dude has serious trust issues. He sees boogeymen where there are none. You can't let his issues become your own. Lead with your own heart, Marky. Promise me that."

Wrapping my arms around her, I am amazed how her translucent skin still allows me to touch her. "But how, Brae? How is this all possible?"

"You're a Prime now baby!" She answers with a cute little wiggle and step. "It's all part of your abilities. Dreams. Visions. The whole gamut."

"Wait, so do you mean I can see you like this from now on? This is great!"

"No, I'm afraid not," Brae softly replies. Her eyes glass, but instead of tears, etchings like a trail of diamonds frame her eyes. "It's okay, baby. At least we have now. But we don't have long."

"Brae, what's going on?"

"This is just a gift, baby. From Damina."

"Damina? But how?"

"When she took on the proxy that night to bind her soul to mine, she gave up her position in the higher place for me."

"What?" I freeze in shock. While I've never outright blamed Damina for succumbing to her curse before Braelyn and I were married, there was a part of me that resented her for yet living while my sweet Braelyn died. Little did I know, she did so at her own peril. Now a cursed soul, she will find no peace in the higher place because she gave up her spot for Braelyn.

I can't help wondering if Jackson knows. I'm sure if he did, he wouldn't bother trying to save my pack, but instead put all his energy into finding Damina. Knowing so many are giving up so much just for me is a heavy burden to bear.

Taking my hands in hers, she squeezes my palms. "And that's why you have to find a way to make this work," Braelyn adds. Shooting her listen-up-dummy-super-serious stare, Brae narrows her eyes and twists her mouth. "Oh and before you ask, yes, I can hear your thoughts. I don't know how, but things seem to work differently here." She laughs, waving around. "But seriously handsome, you have to make this work. You have a bigger part to play in all of this more than you know. So does she."

It doesn't take a genius to know who Braelyn is referring to. Claudia.

Thinking of everything Claudia has done, from breaking my

heart, attempting to kill Jerrica, and to think of it, the rude way she treated Damina, I don't think her curves alone will be enough to make this coupling work.

"But it has to work, Marky," Brae chides, lifting my chin. "Besides when did you ever let the opinions of others sway you? There were tons who thought I wasn't worth a grain of salt, but you doused the noise. That's what this time is for. Dousing the noise. It doesn't matter what anyone else thinks. Trust your heart."

"My heart? Really, Brae! My heart is the last thing I can trust right now. Because it's broken! It broke when you died! How can I trust something that's broken?"

"Well, all I know is, until you loved me, my heart hadn't beat in over two hundred years! I lived because you loved me, Mark. Now it's time you let somebody do the same for you..."

Braelyn!

My heart is pounding like a mad drum when I jump up in a cold sweat.

Looking around and finding myself straddled across this impossibly small full-sized mattress, I can't help how annoyed I feel that I'm not in the same garden-like dream with Braelyn.

Gone are the soft sheets and Braelyn's sweet smile.

Instead, I'm left in this cold hovel, mated to a woman who was probably sent here by her venomous ancestor to kill me. Everyone knows how much Chartreuse hates wolves. So much so that she ensured that same hatred passed down to her descendants, like Colin, Claudia's father. He couldn't stand his precious Claudia having any interest in me.

Douse the noise...

Braelyn's parting words strike a chord in me, and I jump from the bed, sweat dripping down my temple. I need to get out of here!

Tossing the door open, Claudia shrieks, startled, gripping the blanket I tossed at her last night between her fingers. Her eyes grow wide with fear as she stares at me, and a loud roar erupts through me. Fearful I'll shift in front of her or worse, rage about in wolfen form, I bolt from the room.

Swinging the large front door open, another roar pulses through me and I feel my wolf beckoning to be set free.

Braelyn said I have to douse the noise. This is the only way I know how.

Taking one last look over my shoulder at Claudia, my eyes flash and I see its bright reflection mirrored in her eyes as her eyes lock with mine. She gulps, heaving down what I can only make to be a tinge a fear and I huff out another grumble of my own before phasing and exiting the den.

Chapter 12

Nothing compares to this.

How I've gone as long as I have without phasing, I don't know. But goodness knows I needed this. The exhilarating, freeing feeling of bones breaking and bending to marrow is not for the faint of heart, but it's all worth the pain. The colors and textures I see with my wolfen eyes are indescribable. The distinct smells and aromas I detect can only be understood by creatures of nature such as wolves.

For all their predilections, not even Altrinion-vampires can attest to the raw brilliance of nature and the serenity found in the ability to transform into another creature entirely. This is a rare gift afforded to wolves alone, and it's one I wouldn't trade with my entire life.

And for the first time in a while, my mind feels clearer than ever. Instead of the chaotic, grief-stricken thoughts of Braelyn, my mind is focused. Clear.

Memories of the time I spent with Braelyn shuffle through me, but this time it does not haunt me. Rather, I feel fortunate. Blessed. Just the short months we shared give me a sense of peace that perhaps my life was not some colossal mistake after all. What's more, as I replay my dream of Braelyn in my mind, I have a feeling there yet remains a bigger purpose to my life than I ever imagined.

Although my heart still aches at her loss, knowing Braelyn is not suffering a scourge's hell calms my heartache.

But I've also done as my Prime Alpha has encouraged me to do. Trust my wolf.

It's been months since I've heard the harmonious cadence of my wolf's voice still the erratic muddied thoughts of my mind.

How I have missed you, my friend.

I thought for sure my wolf would cuss me out the first chance he got. It's been quite the opposite. Every word he speaks to me is like a healing balm. Quieting the storm brewing in my thoughts, his encouraging words give me hope that despite the chaos around me, all will be okay.

There's only one area where I am still uneasy.

Claudia.

While I don't fear what is to come—even my death—for even then, at least I have hope to reunite with Braelyn, I fear allowing someone else into my heart. Especially Claudia. How can I trust someone who's not only broken my heart once, but also tried to kill my friend?

But I do trust Braelyn. And if she's found a way to vouch for Claudia from the great beyond, I at least owe it to myself to see it through. Besides, my pack is counting on me. I will not let them down!

Breaking from my shift, I yelp aloud as I find myself before the large oak door of the den once again. Rising to my feet, I hold on to the doorframe, slightly nervous to open it. It's been hours since I left, and I didn't account for preparing before my shift. Namely clothes.

Normally I'd put a few clothes near a tree or somewhere

inconspicuous so that I had a change of attire once I was done. Now, however, I'm standing stark naked in front of the door, dreading opening it. Sure I know the whole point of mating requires nakedness, but Claudia and I are nowhere near that comfortable with one another.

Sighing, I grab the doorknob and push the door open. If she has to see me naked so soon, then so be it.

Slowly cracking the door, I peek inside and notice the air feels lighter than before. Still, I'm surprised I don't see Claudia. Stepping over the threshold, my feet ruffle against something soft. Looking down, I'm surprised to find a pair of my shorts folded neatly on the ground. Quickly grabbing them from the floor I put the shorts on and look around.

My eyes widen in surprise noticing the place seems spruced up.

Stepping inside, I am slightly taken aback to find all the cobwebs gone from yesterday.

"Don't look so surprised." Claudia's voice startles me and I turn to see her sitting in the small rocker near the mantle.

"Crap, Claudia!" I snap, shocked. "What are you doing hovering in the corner like a creeper?"

"Um, I'm not the one stalking naked into a wood side cottage. I, on the other hand, am sitting here reading like a normal person does on a Sunday afternoon."

Grunting, I shut the door behind me. "It's Sunday already?"

"Last time I checked," she huffs, shaking the newspaper in her hand and flipping it over, rolling her eyes.

I wonder what's crawled up her butt? I was in a good mood only two minutes ago.

Leaning against the door with my arms folded, I give her a stare. "Claudia, what's wrong?"

"Nothing." She bites her lip and keeps her eyes on the paper.

"Are you sure?" I say annoyed. I should go for another run. I'm not in the mood for this. Then it hits me. "Oh, the shorts? Well, you didn't give me a chance to thank you. I appreciate it."

"The shorts? You think I'm mad about that? Well, sure, I didn't want your ass getting bit by whatever other creepy crawlies we've got running around here—but that's hardly it."

"Okay, then what? This place? Thanks for cleaning it. But I do think it's a bit too soon for the nagging mate routine."

"Never mind, Mark," she sighs. "Anyway, there's food in the oven. We can eat whenever you're ready."

Damn. She cooked too? Who is this woman? I never thought of Claudia as the domestic type.

"Thanks, Claudia but you really didn't have to go through all the trouble."

Standing up, she twists her mouth into a quirky smile before shaking her messy bun loose. Her ginger-laced tendrils fall to her shoulders, framing her silhouette into a softer image than the slight scowl on her face suggests. Something is bothering her, but she doesn't want to talk about it.

Forcing another smile, she places the newspaper on the rocker. "Well, we have to eat, right?"

Looking at her, I'm surprised to find her wearing the cloak from earlier. Rolling up the sleeves, she quickly pats the would-be wrinkles at her sides and saunters across the room.

"I had to rinse out my clothes from all the dust," she adds, pointing to a few of her things near the fireplace. "I was sneezing like crazy."

My stomach rumbles as I notice the food in the oven. Normally my wolf eats some forest catch, but this time we spent more time getting reacquainted with one another. Whatever Claudia made has my hunger on overdrive.

"Thanks again, for going through the trouble," I say, making my way to the bathroom to wash up.

Claudia remains quiet as I splash water on my face and wash my hands. Looking in the mirror, I see her countenance fallen as she pulls the food from the oven, and I wonder what is bothering her.

Twisting her face into a frown, my inner alarm bells ring aloud and I wonder if it's wise eating what she's cooked. I keep my gaze locked on her as I work hard to listen to her breathing. If the pacing of her heart is off in the slightest, it could mean she's nervous. Perhaps even nervous about poisoning me.

"What?" Claudia snaps, looking up at me through an opening in her wavy hair. And while it's kind of sexy to see her bright, green eyes peer through her tresses, I try to keep my lust in check. "Why are you staring at me like you're scared to sit down?"

Her tone annoys me but I don't want to let her know I suspect anything. At least not yet.

"Well, I didn't poison it if that's what you're worried about," she laughs, turning around to put a few things together.

"Should I be worried?" I answer darkly, with my arms folded.

Turning quick on her heel, the way her upper lip curls at the sight of me is both maddening and musing all at once. "Really, Mark? Wow! I can't believe you of all people could think so low of me."

"Yeah, and I never thought you of all people would try to kill Jerrica!" I bite back.

"How many times do I have to—you know what, never mind. I'm not doing this with you." Brushing her hands through her hair, Claudia sighs hard.

"Well, what am I supposed to think, Claudia? They found you with the knife. And yet even now you've said very little to prove your innocence." I huff, leaning against the wooden stool.

Claudia's eyes glass as she stares at me, but she looks away, batting her eyes fast. Looking over her shoulder, she sighs again. "I don't know, Mark. I was hoping my word was enough. At least with you." While her words are barely more than a whisper, the pain in her tone jabs me like a knife to my gut.

Squeezing the back of the chair, my jaws clench as I pry my eyes away from the alluring view of Claudia DeVeaux. Even in that hooded cloak, she looks more delectable than normal. I know I need to mate her, but I've never been more torn than I feel right now.

"Look, Claudia, it's just you're not making this easy for me. I mean, just your bloodline alone is reason enough to call this whole mating business off. But I'm here—"

"My bloodline? You can't be serious!"

"Um, yes I can! Hell Claudia you're the descendant of Chartreuse Grenoble for crying out loud!"

"So? What the hell does that have to do with me? I am my own person—or don't you see me as a person. Because I certainly don't hold you responsible for your bloodline. I mean you are a cursed pack leader, right? And if this doesn't work you'll go back to the bidding of the moon. I'd think a little grace from you would be in order seeing as though I'm helping you out."

Stepping back, I feel my wolf rumble within me. If I didn't know better I'd think he was giving me a gut punch, daring me not to mess this up for him.

Horny bastard.

But both Claudia and my wolf are right. She is helping me out.

"Look Claudia, I didn't mean—"

"No, Mark, you said what you meant. But I'm surprised at you. I never thought you went along with such a double standard."

My brows furrow, and I worry I'm missing something. "What double standard?"

"Oh come on, Mark! Comparing me to Chartreuse? So because she's considered a villain and we're related, that automatically makes me the same?"

"Well no, but even you can agree she's done some scary shit over the years."

"Sure—just like Dalcour, and Decaux—oh and even Jerrica!"

Reeling back from the table, my eyes widen and my jaw drops. "Oh come on, Claudia! Well, maybe Decaux—but Dalcour and Jerrica—absolutely not!"

Laughing, she circles the small space. "Okay, let me get this right, Dalcour—Chartreuse's sire. The Altrinion-vampire who made Chartreuse what she is and who is currently out gorging on blood all because his heart got broke. Oh and Decaux, his brother, the devil of an Altrinion responsible for the Great New Orleans fire of 1788. But I guess all is forgiven since he has a daughter now—one who brought about these rabid creatures that you need me to mate with you just so you have the strength of your pack to stand against. And don't get me started on Little Miss Perfect—Lady Jerrica Jeffers!"

"Enough Claudia!" I shout back. She's made her point. Quite frankly, she's not wrong, but it's also not that black and white. "You made your point. We're surrounded by monsters. You're looking at one."

Claudia's eyes widen, forming glassy pools once more. "No, Mark. You're not a monster. You just want to save your pack. Just like Chartreuse wanted to save her family centuries ago. Sure, she's done some villainous things along the way—but even that has nothing to do with me. I just don't want you looking at me through some villainous lens. I just want you to see me. Because that's the only way this will work."

Staring at Claudia, I can't help being impressed. Not that I'm surprised she's holding her ground, but if she's going to stand at an alpha's side, it's important she takes no crap from anyone. The fact she looks sexy as hell giving me a piece of her mind is a bonus. A bonus that looms at my crotch. I can only hope she can't see me stiffening through these shorts.

Silence sits between us as we both settle our hearts. It's clear she won this round.

Gesturing her hand for me to sit, I pull my chair from the table and plop down.

She sets the food on the folding table, and I'm once again impressed to see she found a way to arrange everything. Using a plaid piece of fabric from what looks like a torn curtain, they lay like placemats while she puts the cast iron in the center. Dividing the food so that there's equal portions on either side for both of us, I'm starkly stunned with how she makes such simple food look like it was chef prepared.

"Khalil taught me how to make steak," she begins, pointing at my plate for me to dig in.

Lifting my brow, her reveal surprises me. She always seemed like she spent more time ordering the cooks and serving staff around than learning from them. "Really? I didn't know Khalil taught anyone his secret recipes."

Twisting her mouth once more, she lets out a small laugh. "Well, in his words, since I spent so much time in his kitchen, he thought I should at least learn how to cook." Hunching her shoulders, she picks around the carrots and potatoes, taking small nibbles.

Scarfing the first few bites of steak, I take notice of her picking and then I remember. "Claudia," I begin, watching her swirl the steak around in the bloody tinge at the bottom of the pan. "Thanks for remembering I like my steak medium rare." Her face lifts in a small smile and she forks a thin sliver in her mouth, nodding her head. "And besides, you know there was never anything wrong with your figure when we were kids, right?" I want to say there's nothing wrong with it now, but it feels too soon.

Claudia's eyes glance to mine and the glassy pools I see there tell me the insecure girl I once fell in love with is still there beneath it all.

"And there's nothing wrong with you now." Her mouth eases into a smile, while her shoulders relax. "So eat up." I laugh, shoving a forkful of steak and carrots into my mouth. Looking at her, I can't help wondering if this may work after all.

Chapter 13

The good news is dinner went without incident. The bad news is, we're already on the second night of the copula and we're nowhere near mating.

Not that I'm truly up to the task, but I know every day that goes by only means either I'll set my pack up for failure or success. Even worse, I know Brian is chomping at the bit, waiting to condemn Claudia for whatever role she played in Jerrica's attempted murder.

I don't blame him.

I mean, I could possibly overlook how Claudia broke my heart when we were kids, because, hell, we were kids, but murder is something else entirely. Sure, Jerrica isn't always the easiest person to be around, but she's been good to me and my pack. Over the years, I assumed Jerrica and Claudia didn't get along because they were equally snobbish to some degree. But I never thought Claudia would try to kill her.

How can I just get over that and mate her?

And while I felt my wolf raging beneath me each time she bit her lip or swept her hair to the side, logic keeps reminding me this woman can't be trusted.

Thankfully after a day of cleaning and cooking, Claudia was pretty beat and decided to turn in early. She remained strangely quiet while we ate. With exception to sharing how long it took her to figure out lighting the pilot light, she kept her conversation minimal. This is very different from the chatty Claudia DeVeaux I grew up with. Then again, this has got to be as odd for her as it is for me.

A part of me feels wrong for laying in this bed while she remains on the couch, but she seems to have made herself at home. Turning the sofa so that it's facing the fireplace, she nestled herself right down into the blanket while I cleaned the kitchen and was snoring away in no time.

It's quieter tonight than I recall of last night, save the trickling sounds of rain from outside. Last night my mind was such a mess, I fell asleep as soon as my head hit the pillow. Tonight, however, listening to the sounds of rain as I count the lines of wood in the paneling is all I can do to stay sane.

No cell phones. No television. This place was designed for one thing and it's that one thing that is the farthest from my mind.

Heavier drops of rain hit against the windowpane and the sharp sounds of thunder rumble through the sky. Strangely, I don't recall smelling any hint of an impending storm when I phased earlier. Something tells me this storm is likely supernatural. While I don't sense any cause for alarm in the nearby vicinity, it's just another reminder why I need to get back to my pack and protect the city. Although I'm thankful for Jackson's help, this is still my territory and it's up to me to defend it.

Once more the thunderous storm rattles through the sky and I feel the den shake. Sharp, crackling sounds of lightning break through the dissonant quiet of our abode, ringing the alarm bells within me.

Hairs along my forearm and neck stand up as a low growl churns through me and I jump up from the bed, throwing my door open. A bright, white light blares through the room as the lightning strikes outside and the den rattles once more. Quickly, my eyes dart to Claudia, tucked away in deep sleep on the sofa. She's totally oblivious to the storm raging about, but my wolf hurls me like lightning to her side.

Scooping her in my arms, I lift her from the couch and run to the bedroom, tossing her on the bed.

Squealing, Claudia jumps up, looking around bewildered. "Mark! What the fu—"

She barely has a chance to utter the words when a large tree trunk falls through the roof, spearing into the sofa.

"Are you okay?" I ask over my shoulder, keeping my eye on the ceiling, fearful of anything else plummeting through.

"I—I—um—yes," her words chatter behind me. "What happened?"

"Bad storm," I say looking around the den. "Are you sure you're okay?" Turning around, I'm not prepared to find her wearing nothing but one of my white tees as she sits on her knees in the center of the bed. I guess now I know what she was wearing under that cloak. With wide eyes, pouty lips, and gorgeously messy hair, she looks like the most deliciously fuckable thing I've ever seen in my life. Her eyes glare over my shoulder at the apparent mess in the main area, but I can't help gaping at the sight of her perky breasts on display or the soft curves of her inner thigh, which only slightly cover my view of her sweet spot. *My, what a sight she is!*

"You—you—saved me?" Her voice is barely audible, but it's the question in her tone more distressing.

Our eyes lock and I feel my wolf buckling beneath my skin,

begging for release. "Of course," I answer.

Claudia keeps her gaze set on me and I see her eyes glass. "After everything? Why?" Loose tears fall to her chin, and I'm surprised how much I want to wipe them away. "I mean, I know you hate me."

"Because despite what you think—or even I thought before now—I can't imagine a world without you in it, Claudia. And no, I don't hate you." I want to tell her I hate how she's got my heart jumbled in knots.

Tossing her face into her palms, she curls into her knees and cries. "But I've been so horrible to you over the years. I wouldn't blame you if you wanted me dead!"

The sound of the storm lessens as does the danger I sensed earlier. Slowly, walking to the bed, I do my best not to let my eyes look behind her. I don't think I can resist seeing every part of her tonight. Rubbing her back, I feel her shiver in my grip and I realize she's genuinely shaken to her core.

I want to hold her. Take away her fears. "Claudia, you're safe now."

Slowly rising back to her knees, her eyes once more lock with mine and I feel the same magnetic pull I did during the ritual. Wrenching my arm around her waist, I yank her close. I feel her nipples graze my chest through the cottony fabric and I feel myself harden, hitting her abdomen. Her eyes widen and her lips part so slow, I take every second to admire just how stunning she looks with nothing but the faint light of the stars illuminating my view of her.

"Mark," she begins, looking at me with such an earnest stare, she could ask me for half of everything I owned, and I'd give her all that and more. "It wasn't me. I did not try to kill Jerrica."

Claudia's words surprise me, breaking me from the lustful

thoughts fueling me. Loosening my grip, she falls back on her legs and pulls the duvet at the bottom of the bed to her chin.

"Then what happened? I want to believe you but—"

"Please just believe me. Look, I'm a lot of things, Mark, but I'm not a killer."

"I want to believe you, but they found you with the knife and then you ran. What do you expect me to think?"

"I expect you to know the girl you shared your first kiss with isn't a killer, despite my family tree. Trust me, I want to tell you everything, but I just need you to trust me. I promise I'll tell you and everyone the truth once we get back with the stone."

Distancing myself, I grunt, hitting the wall. "You're not making this easy for me, Claudia. Or yourself for that matter. If you're found lying with that stone, you'll die! Do you understand?"

"Yes, I know." Her eyes deepen into mine, and I see she's not budging. "I wouldn't risk it otherwise."

"If you're lying, Claudia the fate of my entire pack, Louisiana, and possibly everything we hold dear is at risk."

"That's why I'm asking you to trust me."

"Trust you? That's a tall order, don't you think?"

Swallowing the thick air in her throat, she tosses her hair back, slightly arching her back, revealing her perfect breasts once more. "Then why save me, Mark?"

I want to answer her, but I can't. I'm fighting every urge to tear that shirt from her luscious curves and delighting myself in her in this instant. Clenching my jaw, I work hard to keep my eyes on hers, but it's hard not allowing them to drift lower.

Grunting, I know I need to say something, instead of standing here gawking at her rack and thighs. "I don't know

Claudia. All of this is illogical. I should want you dead. But I don't. I'm not sure if it's the effects of the copula or just the way I feel looking at you right now, but I know one thing I can't let anything happen to you. Now trusting you—"

"Well, you'll just have to work that out if I'm going to be your mate. Besides, I have to trust you too." Her voice is soft as she fidgets with the shirt at the tip of her knees.

Cocking my head to the side, my brow raises, curious. "How so?"

"Well, it's not the stone I'm worrying about killing me."

Lifting her chin to meet my eyes, the glassy puddles I see there make me want to dive deep. "What then Claudia are you worried about?"

"Dying the first time I make love."

A gasp is all I have in response. I've always assumed Claudia was way more experienced than me. Not that it changed the way I saw her, but this new information is changing the way I see *us*.

Chapter 14

"I think we're good," I yell down to Claudia as she steadies the rocker. One more punch, and I bang the nail into wood, ensuring the plank is sturdy. Climbing down, I take one more look at my makeshift patch job and I wince when I notice water dripping inside. "It'll hold for the night, but it's probably not gonna hold long against the water."

"It's okay, we can just pull the couch on the other side. I'll sleep there."

Laughing, I point at the huge tree trunk still impaled through the cushion. "Yeah, unless you want to sleep with a big piece of wood between your legs—um—that didn't come out—"

Covering her chuckle, she shakes her head. "I think I get what you mean." Pacing the floor, she keeps laughing and I feel like I'm missing the inside joke.

"Care to share the joke with me?"

With the duvet still wrapped around her, she keeps it at her chin, slightly shivering from the cold rain. "It's just a wayward memory," she smiles and her cheeks blush.

"I think I could use the laugh."

"Well, do you remember when we all stayed at Trieu's camp that summer?"

"Oh my goodness, you're not talking about *that*, are you?"

Claudia continues laughing, covering her mouth with the blanket. "Yes. That!" Bending at the waist, she leans against the wall. "You woke up with a stiffy, screaming that something was wrong with it!"

"Oh damn, Claudia I was hoping you forgot about that!"

"How could I? You ran down the hall shouting you think you got a splinter of wood in it." Bursting with laughter, Claudia barely holds herself against the wall at the thought of my youthful wiles.

"Well, if my father took time to explain anything fatherly to me, perhaps I wouldn't have freaked out. I guess it's a good thing Brian was there to help me sort everything out. He always seemed like some cool twenty-year-old who drove us around back then, but after that summer at camp, he took me under his wing."

Claudia's laughing stops and a strained glare mars her face. "Yeah, and now that cool guy wants me dead."

Sighing, I inwardly scold myself. I know the topic of Brian is touchy.

Making my way to her, I place my hand on her shoulder, searching her face. "I won't let him hurt you." Claudia's eyes glass, but she tightens her lip, refusing her tears their release. "Trust me." Widening her eyes as she looks up at me, a small smile crinkles the corner of her mouth.

"Still… you and wood?" She laughs again.

Laughing with her, I shake my head. "Okay, okay that's enough fun at my expense."

"Oh, I'm not finished!" Claudia adds, lifting her hand and trying to stifle her laughter. "I've got a few more stories with you and wood, mister!"

My brows crease, curious. Sifting through my memories,

I wonder what Claudia is referring to. "Doubtful," I reply, tugging the branch impaled in the sofa. It's going to take a little more work to pull it out.

"I assure you I have plenty, Lord Helsing," she quips, covering her laugh. "Like the time you tripped over that wooden bench on the stage at graduation. There you were, heading to the podium, when that wretched bench attacked you! It knocked you on your ass if I recall."

The playful sarcasm of Claudia's tone is refreshing. Looking at her now, she reminds me of the girl I fell in love with all those years ago. It's surreal since I was certain that girl was long gone.

Still laughing, she walks behind the couch and firms her hands on both sides. Nodding, she looks at me, gesturing for me to try pulling the branch out, while she sturdies the couch. "No worries, Lord Helsing. I won't let this couch best you like that wooden bench," she laughs.

Straightening her posture, she leans against the sofa, steadying it as I try to work the wood out from the cushion.

Grunting, as I pull the branch, "Well, it wasn't one of my finer moments, that's for sure." Dropping a thick piece of wood on the floor, I step back, frustrated there's still a thick log wedged inside.

"I don't know if I'd say that." Claudia's voice is softer than before as she leans against the wall. Her big, bright eyes beam in my direction, and a small smile curves at the corner of her mouth. "I mean it took a lot of courage to get up from the floor and still give a graduation speech. You even found a way to make a teachable moment out of it. Something about getting back up after you've been knocked down. I think you've proven that over and again in your life, Mark."

My eyes lock with hers and my heart thumps wildly in my chest. "Wait a minute," I begin, thinking back to my graduation. "Claudia, how do you know all of this? I don't recall you being at my graduation."

Claudia's eyes fall as she fidgets with her fingers. "I was there, Mark. I wouldn't dream of missing your big day." I don't know if it's the quietness of her tone or the sincerity in her gaze, but her words are like a balm to an injury long past.

"I—I don't know what to say, Claudia. But your department's graduation was the same day, wasn't it?"

She hunches her shoulders as if it were no big deal. "Yeah, it was earlier. The graduating class for my interior design department was much smaller than yours in sociology. Still, knowing you were giving the address, I just had to be there."

I am speechless. How could I have been so wrong about her all these years?

"I'm sorry, Claudia. I didn't know. Although I wish I'd known you were there, I'm glad you told me."

"It's all right, Mark. We were in different places back then."

Sighing, I round the couch and come to her side. Strumming my thumb along her cheekbone, seeing her cheeks warm at my caress, touches my heart. "But it's good we're here now," I smile, kissing her forehead. Turning her around, I gently push her toward the bedroom. "And now, Miss DeVeaux, we need to get some sleep."

"Are you sure?" Claudia asks over her shoulder, peering up at me through her sexily wild mane.

Damn, this is going to be tough.

"No problem," I lie. This will be harder than I can imagine. And so will I. "You can sleep under the covers, and I'll stay on top."

"Hmm, maybe you should sleep underneath. You're bigger than me, I'll never be able to move. I'll use the duvet."

"Okay, but if you get cold—"

"I'll be fine. This thing is pretty heavy," she adds, shaking the duvet at her chin.

Pulling off my shirt, Claudia quickly turns her back to give me privacy, but not before her eyes scan the length of me. If I didn't know better, I'd say she took in an eyeful of my manhood before averting her gaze. I guess this will be equally as hard for her as it is for me.

"All in," I say, rolling on my side, giving her privacy.

"Okay, no peeking," she whispers.

I keep my eyes on the wall in front of me, but when I see the curves of her shadow against the wall, I feel my primal thoughts take over.

I'm not sure this was the best plan.

"You okay over there?" I ask as I feel her lay next to me.

"Yep, just getting comfortable."

"Got enough room?"

"I'm good, thanks."

Staring at the wall my mind races about, and I wish her sweet pheromones would do anything but beckon me as they are right now. It feels like the ritual all over again.

Silent minutes go by, and her breathing deepens, and I am hopeful she's drifting asleep.

"Mark?" Her voice is small, barely above a whisper.

My eyes widen, surprised she's still awake.

"Yes."

"I shocked you, huh?"

I smile. "Well, yeah, I suppose you did. I never thought it would be your face I'd see when I pulled off the hood of that cloak. I don't know who I thought I'd see, but when I saw you—"

Clearing her throat, she interrupts me. "No, not that."

Confused, I turn over and find her staring at me. "What then?"

Dipping her head into the duvet with a bashful gaze, only showing her eyes. "Learning that I was a virgin."

The thought goes straight to my manhood.

"Well, it was more unexpected is all."

"Why? Because I'm descendent from ladies of leisure like Chartreuse? I know that's what everyone thinks."

"Who cares what other people think."

"I care what *you* think."

Who is this woman? I've never seen Claudia DeVeaux so vulnerable. Ever.

"I've never thought less of you if that's what you're worried about. You're a grown woman, Claudia. What you choose to do with your body or who you choose to be with isn't for me or anyone to judge."

"But I know everyone just thinks I'm some high-fluting huzzy. They're always judging me. Because of the way I look. The way I dress. The way I carry myself. If you're too sure of yourself, you're a bitch. If you're too reserved, you're docile. Women are always judged for something."

Chuckling, I sigh. "You think it's just women? Men are judged no different. My father spent his entire life, jumping in and out of ladies' beds. And just because he did, everyone assumes the same of me. Most think I'm just another party boy, sleeping my way through life with whomsoever will."

Claudia's eyes grow wide, and she lifts her chin above the cover. "I never thought that about you. I mean not that you couldn't get by in life with your looks alone, but I always knew you were nothing like your father."

Her words surprise me.

"Really?"

"Yeah, really. Don't get me wrong, it was hard seeing you with other girls after we broke up but—"

"You mean after you dumped me."

"I didn't dump you, Mark."

Sitting up on my elbow, I frown. If this is going to work, she has to be honest. "Um, let me see if I recall how it went down. Right, I remember. You sent me an email, saying Mark it's over."

"What?" she says, pushing up on her arm. "I never sent you an email, Mark. I came back from Paris and Dauphine said you told everyone you got bored with me. And since you were ignoring me—"

"I never told anyone anything like that. All I recall is Dauphine asking me if I got your email and then—"

"That two-faced wench! I knew she had something to do with it!"

"Dauphine? She wouldn't!"

"Oh she would! She's the one who told my dad we were together and that's why he sent me to Paris for the summer. That explains why when I got back my father told me her parents had arranged for you two to be together. My father said you two were a better fit. And after we started our freshmen year in college it just seemed like we were both headed in opposite directions."

"Now look at us," I laugh, shaking my head at the foolery of it all.

Our gaze grips one another in place and all else goes still.

Every part of me warms with a fervor I had not known until now. But it's the irresistible reach of her wide and hopeful eyes drawing me deeper.

"Yeah, look at us," she breathes back, and once more her pheromones implode my space. Falling on her back, the rise and fall of her chest tempts every bit of my resolve. Sighing hard, Claudia gazes up at the ceiling. "I always thought we'd end up here. Like this."

"You did?"

"I never imagined my first time with anyone except you, Mark." Once more, her words shoot straight to my groin. "So I suppose if I don't survive the mating, at least it will be because I finally got my *ever after*—just not the happily part."

Leaning over her, her trusting eyes gape at me and it's taking all my willpower not to lock my mouth with hers. "Claudia, listen when I tell you, I won't let anyone, not Brian, my wolf—or anyone or thing hurt you. Do you understand me?"

Nodding with her eyes only, her mouth once more falls open and I want for everything to fill it with every part of me.

"Besides, when we mate—when we make love, the last thought on your mind will be dying. I've had enough people die for me. I need you to live for me. When we make love, I need you to want to relive it over and over again. I want you alive and excited to see each day. I want you happy, knowing that every day you live is one more day for us to be together. Is that understood?"

I hardly recognize the man I've become with Claudia DeVeaux, but the primal, possessive, beast within me is intent on building a life with this woman. All else be damned.

"Yes," she breathes back.

The neediness of her eyes pulls me to the brink, and I know I can no longer resist.

Chapter 15

Crushing my mouth to hers is almost as liberating as how I felt when I shifted earlier. Claudia's tongue tethers with mine so seamlessly we feel like one. But it's the feel of her body pressed against mine, sending me in overdrive.

With her hands gripping the back of my neck, she holds me steady as our tongues twist and tie together. Her lips taste so deliciously sweet. I can only imagine how the rest of her tastes. Her body writhes beneath me and the feel of her bountiful breasts grazing my chest, makes me want to rip my shirt from her body, setting them free.

Gently pulling from our kiss, I feel my wolf shifting to the driver's seat, but I know I need to slow things down. I've yet to tell Claudia I'm also a virgin and it's important there are no secrets between us, or the mating won't take. Even more, as odd as it seems, I actually want this to work. I can't take any risks. We have to be in sync.

"What's wrong?" Claudia smiles but casts a worried grin.

"I don't want to take any unnecessary risks with you, Claudia. You understand we have to be in perfect harmony or this—"

"Could kill me."

Our eyes dig deep into one another. We both know we have

to be careful.

"I told you, Claudia, I won't let anyone—not even me—hurt you."

Clenching the sheets at my side, she squirms beneath me. "I want this, Mark. I want you."

Slowly, she pulls the duvet to the side, revealing her thigh.

"Claudia don't." I say, turning my head, fearful of seeing the one part of her I know I can't resist. "If I see that pretty little thing, I won't be able to control myself."

Pulling me back into a kiss, she moans against my mouth and it's the sexiest thing in the world. Taking my hand, she trails my hands along her curves, and I feel myself becoming undone. But when she places my hands at her soft center, the pacing of my heart quickens.

"Touch me," she whines, guiding my finger to her entrance.

The warmth and wetness I feel there, hardens me instantly.

"Are you sure?" I ask, still pressed against her mouth. Sealing her approval with another kiss, she firms her grip on my hands, leading me inside her sweet center. "So tight. So wet," I grunt. "Maybe it's a good idea for me to prime it a bit. Make sure you can take what I have to give like a good girl."

"I'll be your good girl," she coos into my ear.

Slipping my finger from inside, I bring it to my mouth, sucking her sweet nectar from my fingertip.

"Tastes so sweet," I say, running my hand back down to her entrance. "This sweet thing is dripping wet."

"I've been wet all day. It's been torture!"

Then it hits me. "Is that why you were mad at me earlier?"

"Yes, Mark! I've been horny all day. Ever since I heard your roar during the ritual yesterday, I've been on pins and needles."

I knew the mating ritual affected wolves, but I had no idea

how it affected mortals. But it makes sense. That's the whole point of the ritual. Everyone in that place was slaked with lust, I suppose mortals are no exception. Even more, she accepted the mating pronouncement so that means the same magic that runs through my veins is somehow influencing her as well.

"Well, let me help relieve you a little bit."

"Please," she moans, gyrating against my palm as my finger works her spot.

"I'm gonna make you cum and then you're going to go to sleep. You understand me?" My words are jagged as I twist and turn my finger inside her. When I woke this morning, I never thought we'd be here already, but I am so glad we are.

"Yes," she breathes back. Wiggling beneath me, my shirt rides up on her, revealing one of her breasts and I immediately lean into her nipple. Her breast is so full and nipples hard, thoughts of her riding me as they bounce just for me arouse more than my interests.

Pulling the shirt up, her other breast springs free and I'm surprised to see a tattoo of the Dunes crest just above her heart.

"When did you do this?" I gasp, surprised. We talked about her getting a tatt to match my brand, but we were over before any of that took place.

Claudia's cheeks blush, and she bites her nails. "I did it when I was in Paris. I planned on showing you when I got back. It was supposed to be a surprise."

I gulp. I had no idea. "You did this for me?" Twisting my finger in her depths, I push it further.

Moaning, I feel her relax, allowing me to go deeper. "Yes, of course, Mark. I thought I'd show you—you know the first time we—well, you know."

A part of me wants to investigate further, but I don't want to linger on the past. So I plunge my face back to her breasts, grabbing one and sucking the other. Claudia moans as I do, grinding her hips up and tempting my resolve.

The duvet covering her sweet spot, moves a bit, but I keep it still, I don't think we're ready.

"You keep moving like that—you want me to see it, don't you?"

Nodding with her eyes closed, I feel her pulsing along my grip and it's the best feeling in the world. "I'll tell you this, the minute I see it, I'm going in. But this tight spot is hardly ready. Maybe we'll add another finger."

"I can take it," she sighs as I circle my fingers inside her wet center. "Ahh...Mark," she cries out and I feel her hand, gripping my shaft.

Her hands feel so good.

If she's not careful she'll have a load of me on her in no time.

Circling my finger and clenching her spot, she grinds hard against my palm. "Mark!" Claudia cries out and I feel her pulsating center drip down to my wrist.

Continuing her grip on my leading, it doesn't take long for me to follow suit, and I release all that I have along the inside of her thigh. Staring down at her creamy skin, I can only imagine what she'll look like completely bare before me. But I don't have a chance to think on it for long when she dips her forefinger into my release and sucks it from her finger.

"Mmm..." she moans, swirling her finger in her mouth. "Good."

"Ah, Claudia DeVeaux, you're such a tease!" I laugh, falling to my side.

"You should talk," she smiles, biting her bottom lip as she

turns toward me. "But thank you."

I know I'm smiling like an idiot, but I don't care. "No thank you," I exhale hard, trying to steady my breathing. "I didn't know how bad I needed—"

"Has it been that long? Well, I guess since—"

Shit.

Nope. I'm not ready for this.

After what we just did, thinking of Braelyn right now is just too much. Even more, it would also mean telling her I'm not some experienced, prize lover that she may be hoping for.

Sitting up on the bed, I brush my hair back from my forehead. I feel my muscles tense and everything in me wants to sprint from this place.

"Oh, I—I'm sorry, Mark. I just meant that—"

"I need some water." Jumping to my feet, I make my way to the kitchen and grab a bottle of water from the small fridge. Drinking the entirety in one gulp, I toss the bottle into the sink.

Holding the sink tight, a low growl rumbles through my chest, but I clench my jaws, holding it back. I don't want to scare her. Grabbing a towel I warm it under the water and grab another dry towel.

When I go back into the room, Claudia is still how I left her, holding the duvet between her fingers. Her big, bright eyes watch me carefully as I make my way toward her, and I can tell she's rightfully wary of me. She's been around wolves long enough to know how hazardous our tempers can be for mortals. Still, the last thing I need is for her to be fearful of me.

Holding out the towel, I gesture a modicum of permission and she grants a small nod in return. As gently as I can, I wipe my release from her thigh. I'm careful not to expose her sweet spot, knowing despite how torn I feel at the thought of Braelyn, seeing her there will make this moment harder for the both of us than need be.

I'm still standing like a frozen statue after I'm done cleaning her and I see in her eyes I'm testing her resolve. I want to say something, but I don't know where to begin.

Swallowing the dry air in my throat, I lick my lips, just enough to part them to speak. "Claudia, I—"

Narrowing her gaze briefly, she rolls her eyes and shakes her head, sighing hard. "Goodnight, Mark." Turning away from me, she pulls the duvet over her head and remains on her side.

Real smooth idiot. Real smooth.

Great, now even my wolf is pissed with me.

Just when I thought we were making progress, here we go, back to square one.

Chapter 16

I want to make this right.

No, correction.

I have to make this right.

Claudia and I made more ground than just some first base, teenage, make-out session. We made a connection. A connection I never thought we'd have until last night. Last night I found the girl who first made my heart swoon when I was an awkward, greasy-haired kid from the back of the bayou.

I refuse to let her think for one minute our time together was a mistake.

Sure, it's going to take some time for me to get past my grief of losing Braelyn, but since Claudia has agreed to help my pack and be my mate, I at least owe her better from me. She deserves that.

Even more, I know I cannot expect her to trust me with her truth, if I can't do the same. To mate for life trust is a necessary agent to bind us as one.

That's why I hope what I'm doing now will help matters at least a little.

Claudia isn't the only one who learned a little something from Khalil.

Pulling the last strip of bacon from the skillet, I catch a whiff of her scent as she opens the bedroom door and I spin quickly on my heel.

"Perfect timing! Breakfast is ready!" I announce, happy to see her wide green eyes glaring at me from the threshold of the bedroom.

"You made us breakfast?" She asks, wrapped in the duvet, gripping it at her chin. Her wild mane is still a beautiful mess but it's the perfect placement of the freckles she normally conceals, reminding me of the lovely girl who captured my heart long ago.

"Eggs and bacon! Yes, come and eat," I smile back, placing the skillet on the folding table.

"Okay, let me freshen up." Claudia's tone isn't as cheerful as I hoped. I'm sure she's still wary of me, but maybe I can set her at ease.

Still, I'm thankful she doesn't take long in the bathroom and is back in the main area by the time I pour us juice and set the table.

"Everything smells good," she says, taking slow steps toward her seat.

"Thanks, let's eat." I do my best to keep my tone cheerful, I don't want to upset her.

"Look, Mark," she begins, as she slowly lowers herself into the chair. "Last night—"

"First, let me apologize, Claudia," I begin with my palm lifted in caution.

"No, Mark, you don't have anything to apologize for. It's me. I know you're still grieving, and I guess it was just a gut punch to my ego."

Taking her hand in mine, I gently squeeze it. With a guarded gaze she looks up at me and I want to do everything possible to remove the sadness I see in her eyes.

"Claudia, please. Yes, the subject of Braelyn is still tough for me. Frankly, I don't know when or if I'll ever be over losing her—especially not the way I did. But truly, what I fear most is losing another woman I care about. That's why there's something we need to discuss."

"So this isn't just about Braelyn? I mean, I thought you regretted what we did last night."

"Regret? Please! That is the furthest thing from my mind. How can I regret something I've wanted for so long? In fact, just like you, when we were together in our teens, I always thought for sure it would be me and you. That is before our family and friends did whatever they did to break us up."

Her cheeks blush, and she tucks a few wavy strands behind her ear in the cutest way possible. "Well, I guess that's all in the past now." A small smile curves the corner of her mouth, and she picks up a slice of bacon, swirls it in the egg yolk, and starts to eat.

"Listen, Claudia, last night you admitted your truth to me and it's time I do the same."

Holding a small piece of bacon at the corner of her mouth, Claudia casts a fretful stare as her eyes wander from me to the opposite side of the room. "Okay, let's hear it."

"I'm a virgin."

There. I said it. No better way to get the elephant out of the room.

Claudia's mouth forms an O, and she drops the bacon on the table. "You're kidding me?" she whispers back as if there was someone else in the room.

Her eyes grow wide with disbelief as she stares at me and

all my inner-alarm bells ring aloud.

Abort. Abort.

But it's too late. The truth is out there.

Bare. Naked.

"No! You're pulling my leg!" she quips, leaning back in the chair with her arms folded. The duvet falls to her sides and my eyes go straight to the imprint of her nipples beneath my tee. Damn, she's fine.

Still, I work hard to keep my eyes on hers. She has no idea how much I'm struggling here.

Sucking in a breath, my mouth twists to one side. "Nope, I'm afraid, that's my truth."

"But how?" she whispers again with her hand slightly cupping her mouth.

"Why are you whispering? You realize we're in here alone, right?" I laugh.

Tousling her hair away from her face, she sits up in her seat and I can't help enjoying the jiggle of her breasts. She has no idea how incredibly sexy she looks in the morning. I have every inclination to end our shared streak of virginity right here and now.

"Well, I mean, because you're Mark the Alpha of the Beta Primes! No one in a million years would guess that you of all people are a *virgin*." She whispers the last word, like it's a dirty secret.

"Aren't you the same woman who said people judge you because of this and that? Isn't that what you're doing to me right now?" With one brow raised as I regard her, a part of me is serious, and another part of me is slightly amused at her response.

"Yes, you are right, but I mean I was speaking of how people view women."

"And you don't think men get treated the same? Sure, if a woman sleeps around, she may get labeled worse than a guy, but if a man doesn't sleep around, we get the same treatment."

"Okay, and I'm not trying to bring up a sore subject, but what about you and Brae? I thought for sure—"

"You thought wrong."

Claudia's mouth remains parted, but she closes it and bites her lip. Looking away, she picks up the piece of bacon from earlier and shoves it in her mouth. Grabbing another piece, she twines it between her fingers and picks up a glass of juice.

Her nose scrunches as she drinks. "Yuck, pulp," she says, frowning.

"Sorry about that. I didn't have a strainer. But I did squeeze it myself."

She smiles, reaching her hand across the table. "Thank you, Mark."

"You're welcome, Claudia."

"Not for the orange juice. It's disgusting, lukewarm, and has pulp." Her lips curl in her typical stuck-up manner, but her eyes betray her, and I watch her mouth crest into a soft smile. "But thanks for telling me your truth." She squeezes my hand. "We've both made a lot of assumptions about each other over the years. I'm glad to get to know this version of you."

"Ditto." I wink.

Smiling again, she swirls her bacon in the yolk once more and continues eating. "This is good."

I lean back, admiring the beautiful woman on the other end of the table. When we arrived days ago, I never thought this would work. But now, with all our cards on the table, I'm finally beginning to trust both my heart and my wolf.

"Yes, Claudia," A calculating smile dashes across my face, and she returns an equally cunning grin. "This is going to be very good."

Chapter 17

"So what do you think the big deal is about being a virgin anyway?" Claudia blurts, after chewing her last slice of bacon. Folding her arms over her legs, pulling her knees to her chest I can't help noticing how adorable she looks swaddled in that big blanket.

My brow raises. I wonder where she's going with this. "What do you mean?"

"Well, I mean look at us, we're only twenty-two and it's as if people think by now, we should've had sex with twenty people by now."

"Twenty!" I exclaim, laughing. "I haven't even had five girlfriends—let alone an opportunity for twenty partners." I shake my head at the thought.

With a dismissive wave of her hand, Claudia turns her head. "Oh please, Mark! I know for a fact you've had no lack of girls throwing themselves at you over the years. We may not have been close, but I still had a ringside seat to the parade of dames darkening your door."

I can't help but laugh. "I thought we agreed to set aside our assumptions. Sure, I admit I've always been flirty—"

"Flirty? Is that what we're calling it now. Yeah, okay."

"Okay, Ms. DeVeaux, two can play that game. You don't

think I noticed how you sashayed your ass all across New Orleans over the years, turning heads left and right." A tinge of jealousy rises in me as I recount the swarms of drooling perverts eyeing her. I know one thing; I'd gladly end any who would try today.

Hugging her knees, I see a blush of red fill her cheeks. "And what about you, Lord Helsing?"

"What about me?" I drag my words. It's all I can do to keep my mind from thinking of all those SOB's ogling her over the years.

"Did I turn your head?" Her voice is small. Quiet. But it's the intensity of her stare right now, rekindling the burning I feel inside for her.

"I think you already know the answer."

Twisting her mouth to a small smile, she rolls her eyes and laughs.

"But I'm serious, Mark. Being a virgin is no big deal to me. If that's what you're worried about. It doesn't change how I see you. If anything, it makes me happier that I waited—for you."

Damn. What the hell is she doing to me?

The feelings I'm feeling. Logic says it's too soon to feel like I do. But logic be damned. I want this woman.

But there's still the elephant in the room.

"Listen, Claudia, I wish I could say I was waiting for you but—"

"It's okay, Mark. I understand you and Braelyn were in love. Believe it or not, I was happy for you."

And once again, she amazes me.

"You were? You and Dauphine were so quick to leave the mansion after Brae and I became an item, I thought for sure—"

"To be honest, I was probably happier that you weren't with Dauphine. *Bitch.*" With the way Claudia's lips curl and her eyes narrow, I now see she and Dauphine weren't the bosom buddies I had assumed.

"Claudia!" I admonish. "Now come on, it's not nice to speak ill of the dead."

Hunching her shoulders, she pouts her lips. "Look, I hear you, but Dauphine of all people knew how I felt about you. So seeing her pursue you knowing damn well you were all I wanted, I can't forgive her for that. At least Braelyn and I weren't friends. Her motives were pure, and she truly loved you. Dauphine on the other hand, was a manipulative heifer. I won't apologize for hating what she did to me."

Jumping up from her chair, Claudia paces across the room and looks up at the patchwork and hole in the ceiling. Making my way toward her, I'm surprised to find her eyes glassy with tears. This is more upsetting for her than I realized.

Blinking her eyes hard, she wipes a few loose tears from her chin and turns her head away from me. Taking her shoulders in my hand, I bring her around to face me. Slowly, she locks her gaze with mine.

"I'm sorry, Claudia. I had no idea you felt that way. I really thought you wanted nothing to do with me."

"And so you moved on with Dauphine? My friend? Really Mark?" Huffing aloud, Claudia circles the floor, before turning back to look at me. "Did it ever dawn on you that perhaps the reason I seemed bitchy all the time was because you moved on with her? I mean, damn Mark, it felt like you were really trying to hurt me."

Damn. How did I not think about how this would hurt her before now?

"You're right. That was wrong of me." Deepening my eyes into hers, I search her face, hopeful she believes me. "Sure, I could say that I did what I did out of my duty to the pack but the point is I was wrong. I thought I had to have the resources Dauphine's family provided to ensure my pack would be set, but I never gave a thought to how you might feel. I suppose a part of me felt vindicated because I thought you didn't want anything to do with me."

"But that's the furthest from the truth, Mark. All I wanted was you." Claudia's hazy glare casts a spell on me and all I want to do is hold her.

Pulling her into my embrace, she rests her head on my chest and it's the best feeling ever. She lets out a few small sobs, but keeps her body pressed tight against me. Even through the blanket, the feel of her soft curves sends fervor straight to my manhood.

I could hold her like this all day.

Lifting her head up and out of the cavity of my hold, her bright, wide eyes beam up at me.

"But I'm not innocent in this either," she starts as loose tears trail her cheek. "I should have told you how I felt, Mark. In all reality, I can't blame Dauphine or anyone else for not doing what I should have done. So that's all on me."

"No it's all on *us*," I add, brushing her tears aside with my thumb. "You're my mate now, Claudia. There's no you. No me. Just us."

She smiles. "Just us," Claudia quietly repeats. Shaking her head, she lets out a small chuckle. "Why didn't we say anything to each other sooner. I mean, look at all the time we lost. I mean all of this over an email, really?"

Narrowing my eyes, I pull her back into my embrace.

"Hmm… it probably has something to do with us being kids." I laugh. "Yes, we both should've dug deeper, but to be honest I always felt a little insecure about our relationship back then."

Claudia's eyes widen in surprise as she leans back. "You? Insecure? That's hard to imagine, Mark."

Shrugging my shoulders, I let out a small laugh. "Now see, there you go making assumptions about me again. You don't think guys can be insecure?"

"Well, guys yes. But you, no. I mean really, Mark what could you have to be insecure about?"

Stepping back, I wave my hand through the length of her. "Have you looked in a mirror lately? You're remarkably beautiful, Claudia. And I'm not just saying that because of the copula. You've always been the prettiest girl in the room—hell, in the world. But you always carried yourself so strong and sure. Back then I just hoped I lived up to all that you are. So when I got your email, I figured that was the final nail on my coffin. I thought I was just lucky enough that you settled for a raggedy wolf like me for the short time we were together."

"Raggedy? Settle?" Claudia gasps, wrapping her arms around my waist. "Mark, I was the insecure one. I was the lucky one to be with you. I mean, look at you! Tall. Brawn. Dark wavy hair with flecks of gold highlighting your perfect jawline," she coos, running her hands through my hair. She's giving me goosebumps with just the slight touch of her hand. "Not that it isn't enough you've got these steel-plated abs, but it's this freaking sexy new beard of yours driving me wild!" Claudia exclaims, pulling at the thick hair on my chin. "I mean, damn, Mark you could literally have your pick of the liter."

"But I don't want the liter, Claudia. I want you. So does my wolf. This was always meant to be. I know that now." Tugging my arm around her waist, I pull her so that our bodies touch. "And even though we lost time together, I couldn't be more thankful that somehow, we found our way back to each other. Except this time, we're all grown." Adding a small kiss on her forehead, I let my lips linger before releasing her from my grip.

Smiling wide, Claudia tosses her hair over her shoulder. "I guess we're all grown up now."

Blowing out a hearty sigh, I lean back, keeping my hands on her shoulder. "Woah, well, I guess we both had a lot to get off our chests. That's good—this is good. If this is going to work, it's important that we trust each other. This is a good start."

Claudia's eyes rise, then fall once more. "But that's just it, Mark, I need you to trust me."

"What are you talking about, Claudia?"

"I need you to trust me when I say, I did not try to kill Jerrica."

There goes the other elephant in the room. This one can no longer be ignored.

Stepping back, I allow a bit of separation.

"Listen Claudia, I want to believe you. But you need to tell me what happened that night."

"You deserve an answer. You deserve the truth. And believe me, I'd like nothing more than to tell you everything. But I'd rather wait until I have the stone. That way—"

"Claudia, that stone could kill you if you're found lying! Do you understand that?"

She steps back further. Sucking in a breath, she clasps her hands together, squares her shoulders and darts me a narrow gaze. "Then that is the risk I take!" Her eyes alone plead with me not to pursue this any further.

If this were a week ago, I wouldn't give a rat's ass about a stone. I'd force every lick of truth from her until she begged for mercy. But since the copula ritual commenced, the thought of anyone, including me, hurting Claudia rips my soul to shreds. I'll never let anyone, not even me, cause her an ounce of harm.

"No, Claudia. It's the risk we both take," I counter, closing the distance between us.

Her expression softens, and she sighs before reining in a breath. "I just want you to trust me like you trusted the girl you fell for all those years ago. She's still in here, Mark."

Taking a few more steps, I grab her hand and pull her back into my arms.

"I know, Claudia. I'm looking right at her."

Dipping her head low, I quickly lift her chin, forcing her eyes to lock with mine.

"I'm sorry, Mark. You're putting a lot on the line for me. I know this. I'm hardly worth all of the trouble. Goodness knows I'm far from perfect."

Guiding my hand to the nape of her neck, a low grumble rumbles through me. Leaning back, I search her face and the doubt I see in her gaze troubles me.

"Let me stop you there, Claudia. Who said you had to be perfect to be worth it? Trust me, beautiful, when I tell you this: You are worth it and then some."

Claudia leans deep into my chest, tightening her small arms around my waist, as if she feared I'd disappear. Holding her close feels so good. I never want to let her go.

Pulling back a bit, Claudia tugs my beard and kisses my chin. That has to be the sexiest thing ever. If she keeps this up, I know I'll never cut my beard.

"Okay, so back to the virgin thing," Claudia begins, shyly looking up at me through her thick lashes.

"What about it?"

"Well, you seemed to be worried that us being virgins would negatively affect the mating ritual. Do you think the wolf will reject me because of it? I mean because I really don't know how to fix that besides—"

Gripping her firm ass, I growl. "I can tell you what you're not going to do. You're not giving away what's mine to anyone!" I bark my words and Claudia's eyes flutter and she stumbles back slightly.

"No, Mark that's not what I was suggesting at all," she counters, with her hand lifted in caution.

I work to control my breathing when I realize I'm almost out of breath, enraged at the thought of anyone else with her.

"Oh?" I grunt, loosening my grip but keeping my hand steady. I have no idea where this is going.

"I was just thinking that perhaps we should try a few things—you know to test our comfort levels."

An appreciative smirk crowds the side of my mouth and I scratch my beard. "I'm listening."

"I mean I know last night we got pretty comfortable with one another so at least we have a starting point.

"So what are you suggesting?"

Untying the blanket, Claudia allows it to fall to the ground.

My eyes nearly pop out of their sockets, and I swallow the dry air in my throat as I gaze at her.

Clad in just my tee that barely covers the sweet place I long for, my eyes drag the length of Claudia's perfectly curvy frame. From the view of her large breasts peering beneath my shirt, to the swell of her hips, jutting out at her sides, to her sweet, round face and bright eyes, I am lost in the entirety of her.

"How about a little game of truth or dare?"

Everything in me wants to throw her down to the ground and drive myself deep inside her. I could care less about whatever little game Claudia wants to play, but I'll be a good sport.

"What are the rules?"

"It's simple. We both have to be truthful about our desires and needs."

"And the dare."

"We both dare the other to resist."

Okay, perhaps I'll enjoy this game after all. "All right, Ms. DeVeaux. Game on."

Chapter 18

"Well, you have my attention. But before we begin, I think we should take this to the bedroom. I still don't trust my patchwork," I say, pointing above our heads.

Claudia nods, her cheeks rosy, and I take her hand in mine. Reaching the threshold, I turn and take her face in my hand, guiding her eyes to mine.

"Are you sure about this?" I ask.

Nodding with her eyes only, she smiles. "I've never been more sure about anything." Her trusting eyes deepen into mine and I pull her face close and crush my mouth to hers.

The sweetness of her kiss has me in a tailspin. As our tongues tug and pull, the sweet caress of her lips against mine breathe new vitality into the shell of a man I'd become in my grief. Now, with Claudia in my arms, all I want to do is remain tied and tethered to her in every way.

Slowly, I pull from our kiss, strumming my fingers along her delicate jawline. Kissing the crown of her head, the scent of her pheromones fills my nostrils, causing my wolf to buck within me, raging to be set free.

"Okay, sweetness, how would you like us to begin? But before you answer, I have one stipulation."

"What is it?"

"I'm not penetrating you yet. At least not right now."

Claudia's mouth parts and she scrunches her nose. "As much as I hate to crush my ego, can I ask why?"

"Well for starters, intimacy is more than me shoving myself deep inside your tight little hole."

Her face blushes red and I can almost smell her arousal heighten.

"I'm listening." Claudia's words are wispy, barely audible.

Lifting her arms above her head, I grip her tight at her wrists, leaning her against the wall. "I want to explore your sweet body," kissing her neck, "inch" and moving to the opposite side, "by inch."

She moans, rising to the balls of her feet as my free hand trails down her waistline and back up to her breast.

"Truth or dare. If I kiss you here, will you burn or melt?" I ask, pressing my thumb against her nipple. "Come on, sweetness, I dare you to say this doesn't feel good."

Claudia's body swerves along the doorpost and I do my best to keep my eye on her breasts.

"Ahh, I'm melting Mark," she whines. "Yes, it feels so good."

With her still in my grip, I lead her to the bed, and she sits still, her eyes locked on my shorts. I know she sees how hard I am, but she has no idea I am only just beginning.

"Let's get you out of this shirt," I say, and she lifts her arms, allowing me to remove the shirt. "Damn, you are perfect."

Looking at her perfectly round breasts and the way her hips sweetly spread at the sides makes me feel like I don't deserve something so perfect so soon.

Lifting her chin so that she's no longer locked on my girth, my thumb presses along her lips. But I'm not prepared for her to pull it in and begin sucking.

"My turn," she whispers, as she licks around my nailbed. Bringing my forefinger to her mouth, she licks it as well, alternating sucking. "Now tell me the truth, Mark, would you rather I be sucking something else."

A grunt is all I have in reply and my manhood responds, nearly leaping out of my shorts.

"Well?" she asks with a sly smile.

"Yes," I grit out. "And you'll have an opportunity soon enough."

"Promise?" she smiles, taking my hand in hers. I nod in reply, my gaze hooded with desire. "Cross my heart?" she adds, placing my hand on her breast once more.

"Ahh, so my sweetness likes when I touch these, huh?" I smile as I use both hands to work her breasts. "So big. So beautiful"

Tilting her head, her back arches and it only heightens the view of her perfect curves.

"Lay back." I order.

She does as I instruct and my leading hardens, standing stiff. How the hell did I lay next to her last night and not delight myself in her? I know I just told her I wasn't going in, but that was before I laid my eyes on the prettiest pearl I've ever seen.

Claudia's bare, but her creamy flesh is glistening with her arousal. Slick and ready for entry.

"Tell me the truth, Claudia. Do you want me to taste you now?"

"Please," she cries out, writhing beneath me.

With my hand on her knees, I spread her legs wide, and all the world goes silent. "I'm gonna give you some special kisses for being such a good girl."

"I'll always be your good girl, Mark."

"Yes, you will. And once I've had my full, I dare you not to cum. I dare you not to pour your fountain on me. Let me drink all of you."

Only moaning in reply, her legs open and I lean in, inhaling her sweet scent. It doesn't take long before my tongue is surfing the waves of her nectar as I nibble at her sweet spot. Claudia's hands grip my hair, but only enough to keep me in place.

She tastes so good. Like vanilla and strawberries. Wild and sweet.

Flicking my finger against the same sensitive spot I discovered last night, I take this time to look up between her legs. Her eyes are clinched tight, but it's the sight of her strumming her nipple, reinvigorating my desires.

"My sweet, horny girl," I whisper against her entrance. Lapping her depths once more, she gyrates against my face and it's the most pleasurable experience ever. "Are you ready to cum, sweet girl?"

"Mm… yes," she moans. "Please, Mark, please."

Gliding my tongue along her center, I use my free hand to part her at her sides, working my finger inside. "Let's see if you can take my tongue and finger."

Crying out, the mewling noises Claudia makes as soon as my finger enters her lets me know I found a new spot.

"Oh Mark!" she shouts, her hand pulling at my hair hard.

"Come on, sweetness, let your fountain pour over me. This pretty little pearl is begging for a release!"

Strong, passionate convulsions stir through her as she cries out and her sweet nectar floods my mouth and beard. Her pulsing center squeezes my finger and tongue so tight I wonder how I'll ever get my leading inside.

Panting, she hums, still strumming her nipple in a melody so sweet, it's like a siren to my soul. Planting a few kisses along her inner thigh, I take a moment to appreciate the perfectness of the woman laying beneath me.

Gripping my shaft, I rub my hardened member against her sweet spot. Just the feel of her plump, glistening, flesh against my tip makes me want to dive in. It feels so good just to feel her like this, I fear I'll cum right now. As much as I want to rutt myself deep in her tight hole, I rein in my desire. I need to get my wolf in check before we take this leap. The last thing I want is for anything to go wrong when we make love for the first time.

"What about you baby?" Claudia asks, gazing up at me with a hazy glare. "It looks like you could use a release of your own." Her eyes trail to my waistline and back up to my eyes.

Smiling at her, I can hear in her voice that she's tired. I want for nothing than to forge myself deep, but I have to wait. Dropping back, I pull myself away from her. "It's okay, I can wait. I know you're tired."

"But—"

"But nothing," I say, leaning over her and planting a small kiss on her forehead. "Get some rest. You played hard. I'll need you to save your strength for what comes next."

Casting a hooded gaze, her eyes drift over me. "What Mark? What comes next?"

"Me," I breathe, pressed against her mouth. I give her another kiss. This time I give her perfectly pouty lips the attention they need.

Claudia's eyes widen, attentive. As her hands graze my face, she tries to pull me in for another kiss. My sweet horny girl doesn't want to wait.

But she'll have to. At least for a little while longer. I want to do this right.

With a half-grin, I rise to my knees, admiring my beautiful mate. I couldn't be more thankful than I am in this moment. Soon, I plan to show her just how thankful I am.

Chapter 19

Claudia drifts asleep just as I anticipated. I knew she was tired. And whether she understands it all now or not, I meant it when I said I need her at full strength before we make love for the first time.

Wolf mating can often be a full twenty-four-hour ordeal. Or at least that's what I've been told.

I've known of wolves who couldn't stop having sex for nearly a week after they married or mated. While I know our time may be limited with the copula, I fully expect my more than lust-fueled wolf to make his debut some grand event.

From the way he's been raging to be set free like a caged bird in my soul, I know without a doubt our lovemaking will be stuff of legend.

That's why I need this time for me. I need to shift. Stretch all four legs.

I can feel his restlessness chomping at the bit. So much so, I feared he'd rear his beastly self just as I entered her soft center. Wolves are savage. Even my own. There's no way I'll risk her safety when we make love. I'll not be careless with her.

After draping her with a few blankets and ensuring the patchwork was still holding firm, I left her a note. I let her know I needed to run and to expect me back in an hour or so.

Hopefully, it will give her time to rest or perhaps even weigh her options. If she ever needed an opportunity to leave me and forfeit being my mate, now is the chance. Because when I return, I'll never let her out of my sight again.

The last time I shifted was pure adrenaline. While it may have helped settling my rage and grief, I knew I needed this time to just let my wolf run wild.

And run wild he does.

Since being pronounced as alpha I've changed. I'm a bigger wolf now than I was before. My usually light gray coat is now more white with a gray underbelly and ears. My snout is more blocky and my tail thicker. I'm wider and taller than before and even my paws leave deeper indentations in the earth as I move about.

The cowl of my call is more tranquil than the yelping howl I had grown accustomed to. I sound like my father. Whiplash of bastard he may have been, but he carried the distinction of an alpha's call just as clear as any. Even so, it's strange hearing the similarities in my own call.

I've shifted with Jackson before, and his tone is the same. Alphas by nature carry a more melodic tone than other wolves. A sound made to soothe the savage beast. Now that same melody rests in me.

Running through the wooded lot, I'm amazed at the detail I see with my newly primed wolfen eyes. Sure, I've always been able to see great distances and pick up scents miles away. But since I was stripped of the Dunes curse and reestablished as a Beta Prime, I am now afforded all the abilities Prime wolves have.

Incredible strength and speed are just the tip of the iceberg. But as a prime the call of my yowl speaks to all creatures of nature. Both birds of the air and beasts of the field are subject to the call of a prime.

Every animal I've passed as I made my way through the woods has made some gesture or semblance of respect and submission. Even two small foxes threw their dinner of rabbit at my feet when I came near. They even seemed surprised when I kicked it back to them in return, thankful to resume their feast.

Nearing the edge of the lot, the wind carries a strange scent and I decide to check it out. I've never smelled anything like it before. It smells like a Scourge vampire but this new stench reeks of decay.

My nostrils flare and my tail stiffens at the putrid odor, and I know if I were in mortal form, I'd vomit. I've never smelled anything so vile in my entire life. There's an eerily disturbing mood shifting over me and a sense of threat boils in my blood.

The crackling sound of leaves turns my attention to a row of shrubbery, and I dig my forepaws deep into the earth beneath me yet keeping my hindlegs just atop the ground in case I have to spring into action.

A low guttural sound, like that of murmuring, catches my ear and I keep my eyes forward, as the threat grows near. Just then, a creature, resembling that of a man, wobbles like a drunkard out from behind the shrubs with its hands leering toward me. Warily, I step back. The creature presses forward, lunging at me, but is caught in the bush.

Looking at the strange thing before me, I grow curious. It's clothed like a man, wearing a business suit and even a matching tie. Although that is where its resemblance to a man ends. With a face oozing in boils, tattered skin, and dark, sunken, soulless eyes, this thing is anything but a man.

Still leering at me, it works hard to try to free itself from the bush but seems to have no mental capacity to use logic to do so. I've never seen anything like it. Even Scourge vampires can compute a strategy to attack, this creature seems to have none.

Roaring, I take a step forward, wondering if this creature responds to my call, but it doesn't. It just continues lunging forward with its mouth open and drooling with thick saliva. However, this is no mere saliva. I watch in horror as the searing spital burns a hole straight through the roses on the bush.

I don't have long to investigate this cringy sight before I am yanked from behind. Turning abruptly, I kick my hindlegs hard, freeing myself. Circling back, I see another creature, this one just as decrepit and mindless as the first. Although, without the entanglement of the shrubbery, this one is free to attack.

The first fiend caught in the brush, grumbles aloud, seemingly more enraged at the sight of its counterpart as it works hard to break free. Still, the newly emerged creature keeps its arms reaching for me, panting desperately to have me in its clutches.

Releasing a loud yelp, I send a squalling howl, hopeful to alert nearby creatures. I am thankful when the two foxes from earlier make their way to flank my sides. Both snarling at the monstrous beasts before us. Yipping at the feet of the creature, the smaller fox is seared by the drool of the second creature and caught in its grasp.

To my horror, the creature tears into the foxes' abdomen, feasting on its flesh. The larger fox yaps a loud a wailing sound, and retreats, running deeper into the woods. I don't blame him.

The sight of the creature delighting itself in the fox's carcass gives the first creature motivation to claw its way out from the shrub and it reaches its grimy hands toward me. I work hard to keep myself away from any of its drool as I seek an exit strategy.

All I can think of is keeping these things away from Claudia. I'll never let them harm her. They'll have to kill me first.

Roaring aloud, I stomp my forepaws into the ground, shaking the small trees at my sides. Once more, I stomp, this time harder. The first tree falls onto the feasting creature, crushing its body under the weight of the tree. With another low growl, I stomp harder than before and the tree falls. But it misses the creature, and the gangly fiend lunges for me.

All I see is its slimy drool hitting just shy of my paws and the next thing I see is thick black blood splattered before my eyes. A large katana blade comes in my view as the head of the fiend is severed from its body. As it does, the body is lit aflame and burns to the ground.

Looking up, I see Baxter LaCroix, sweeping his blade across the grass. I hear a loud thump behind me, and I see Bailey LaCroix jumping down from a tree limb as he slices his blade through the other creature, chopping off its head and it too burns.

"My lord," Bailey begins, with a bow at his waist. "We're sorry these two made their way to you."

"Are you okay, my lord?" Baxter asks, while kicking dirt over the flaming husks of the creature.

As much as I want to remain in wolfen form, I shift back into mortal form. Thankfully, wolves aren't squeamish at nakedness. It's certainly common to see the mortal body in all forms. Besides we have a head and shoulders courtesy among dens. Never let your eyes wander below the shoulders and you'll be fine.

"What were those things?" I bark back, worried that these creatures came so close to Claudia.

"Those are the new breed of evil, my lord. The rabid fiends are the closest thing to a zombie we've ever seen. These are what become of any bitten by the vampires recanted by Dacari Peyroux," Bailey replies.

Crap! This is what Jackson was referring to! I can't believe this is happening in my city! It's bad enough to have Scourge vampires roam about, but even they have a modicum of propriety. These creatures know nothing of the kind. And to think these all came to be at the hand of Brian's mate. How can he even begin to point a finger at Claudia when just the words of his beloved made these things?

What a hypocritical ass! He's still my dude, but I'm gonna rip him a new one when I see him again.

"Don't worry, my lord," Baxter continues, with his blade rested at his side. "Dranoel brought Melvina to put up a border around the territory. These were the only two that made it through before our sweep. Lord Nashoba sent more Guardians to the post as well. You and your mate will be safe. We'll see to it."

Bailey nods in affirmation, pounding his fist across his heart.

While I am thankful for their swift action and steadfastness, there's only one person on my mind.

Claudia.

Chapter 20

Shifting back into my wolfen form, I use every ounce of my new speed to make my way back to the den. As I do, I check every corner, taking in copious amounts of air, hopeful I won't detect the rank odor of the rabid fiends.

I am thankful when I make it back to the den and everything surrounding our keep seems just as it's always been. Yet, something seems different. There's a new sheen glistening the entirety of the doorpost that I never noticed. I don't take long to investigate it, as it is slightly reminiscent of the iridescence I recall from before.

It must be the keenness of my new alpha eyes.

Returning to mortal form, I open the door and am once more greeted by shorts at the entrance. I smile at the thoughtful gesture. But I have no intention of wearing them this time around.

Closing the door behind me, I look over to the rocking chair to see if Claudia is there, but she is not. My eyes dart straight to the bedroom, but the bed is made, and I don't see her there either. Quickly scanning the area, I don't see her in the kitchen or near the fireplace.

When I hear the sounds of water to my right, the quick pacing of my heart settles, knowing she is in the bathroom.

I hear the shower running and thoughts of her naked and dripping wet go straight to my manhood.

Before I make my way inside the bathroom, I head to the fridge and grab a bottle of water. Between my shift and tussle with those vile creatures has me thirsty. Chugging down a bottle of water, I'm surprised to see an arrangement of strawberries and fruit on the small plaid pieces of fabric I'd seen earlier inside the fridge. I smile at the thought of Claudia making preparations for us.

I'd never thought of her as the homemaker type. And while I have no expectations that Claudia DeVeaux will ever be a docile mate, it's comforting to know she even cares to make this hovel a home.

Just as I slurp down the last of the water, the hair on my forearm stands stiff and all my inner alarm bells ring once more.

Claudia's loud scream from the bathroom sends a shuttering pulse through me I've never known. Dropping the bottle on the floor, I dash across the room. Thoughts of those salivating beasts pawing their hands on her send me into a frenzy. Although the bathroom windows are not bigger than portholes, I don't put it past the vile fiends to claw their way inside.

Her screams pierce my ears and I'm ripping the door off the hinge in no time.

Standing at the threshold, I look and see Claudia balled into a knot in the corner of the bathtub. Looking around, I see no one, but she continues screaming.

"Kill it! Kill it!" she hollers, pointing at the shower head.

Looking up, I see a large, black, furry spider. Blowing an air of relief, I chuckle and pound my hand against the wall.

Growling hard, the spider obeys the lilt of my call and scurries out of the porthole.

"It's okay, baby," I whisper, hopeful to calm her worry. "He's gone."

"Are you sure?" Claudia says, looking up at me through her soaking wet lashes. "How do you know he won't come back?" She's still balled in a knot, but even curled up she's giving me an eyeful of everything I plan to claim as mine in just a few minutes.

Leaning down to lift her in my arms, I kiss her forehead. "Because I told him not to."

Her eyes narrow, slightly confused. "And you think he'll listen?"

Using my elbow to push in the nozzle to stop the water, I keep my eyes on Claudia. "He better."

"Oh I wasn't finished my shower. I still need to wash my hair."

"Later." My words are quick as I carry her back to the bedroom.

"But—"

"But it's time."

Laying her down on the bed, the sight of her naked and wet body stiffens my leading to full attention.

"Oh," she whispers, her eyes wide and locked with mine.

Gripping my rock-hard shaft, all I can think about is getting inside her. "Are you ready for this?"

"Yes, more than ready," she answers, sitting up on her elbows, licking her lips.

"Listen Claudia, what we're about to do, I've never done this with anyone. Do you understand?"

She nods, blinking her eyes rapidly as she bites her bottom

lip.

"The mating ritual can take a while I'm told. At least until the imprinting takes place."

"Imprinting?"

"Yes, that's when my wolf imprints on you. Marking you as mine. But not only that, it's a transference of power."

"But I don't become a wolf, right?"

I smile. "No, beautiful. But my power will become yours. And since I'm a prime that means my speed, and even some of my strength. You won't shift or phase with the moon, but you'll be my equal in every way. You'll be my mate for life. Is that what you want? Tell me now if this sounds too much for you. If you say—"

"I love you, Mark."

Claudia's words freeze me in place.

"I love you, Mark," she repeats. "I've always loved you. It's okay, you don't have to say it back. But I want you to know I want a life with you. As your mate. And hopefully one day as your wife. For as long as you'll have me."

Damn. She just melted my heart.

After losing Braelyn, I never thought I'd feel like this again. Especially so soon. But this is different. I never mated Braelyn. Claudia, however, is my mate. Our souls are tied and tethered in a way that can't be explained by any mortal known language. The patois of my wolf's call can only be heard by one he considers his equal and no one else. I know now, with all certainly that someone is Claudia.

It's always been Claudia.

Growing up, I heard folk say you only get one great love of a lifetime. Well, I must be the luckiest bastard in the world, because I've found love twice.

"Look, Mark, I know as a wolf, you have to hear the words. You need to hear me grant consent. So yes, Mark, I consent to being yours in every way. I love you."

Crawling on the bed, I hover over her. "Claudia, I never expected this moment to ever come. But I am so glad it did. All I can think about is making love to you. But even more, I can honestly say, I never stopped loving you. And I promise you I'll never stop loving you." I smile, lifting her chin so that her eyes meet mine. She smiles back, and it melts my heart. "Now you've said the words, I need to show you just how much I love you."

Claudia reaches down and grabs my leading, lining it up at her entrance.

"Show me."

Chapter 21

Crushing my mouth to hers, I grip the back of her head, holding her steady. Once more, her sweet tongue collides with mine as her luscious lips lap everything I have to give.

Her body writhes beneath me, and the feel of her breasts grazing my chest hairs sends fervor throughout my body, reinvigorating parts of me I never knew were dormant.

Gripping my shaft, I tease her entrance and am delighted when her bountiful spring drenches my tip.

"Ahh…nice and wet for me," I croon in her ear, nipping at her lobe. I never knew it would feel this good.

"Always," she moans, gyrating her hips, trying to pull me in.

"It's gonna hurt, sweetness," I whisper, kissing her neck. "But I need you to take it like a good girl."

Letting out a small whimper, she rolls her hips. "I'll take it all for you, Mark."

Running my hand down her stomach, I grab her sweet spot hard, tapping my finger at her entrance. Nuzzling the crown of me inside, I press my finger around, opening her wider and her juices run down my finger.

"Does that hurt?" Damn. She feels so good. I hope it doesn't hurt because I'm not coming out.

Wincing, Claudia moans, shaking her head. "It feels good. Don't stop."

Looking at her, my heart pounds within me. We spent so many years apart, I never imagined we'd end up here. Peering at me with her beautiful eyes, a small smile curves at the corner of her sexy lips and my heart thumps once more.

Releasing a low growl, my wolf bucks within me to be set free. Claudia wiggles a bit beneath me, and I can tell the resounding cadence of my call speaks straight to the core of her sweet spot as more of her nectar washes over me.

Priming her opening with my tip as I feel myself ready to sink inside her, I know it's time. There's no going back now.

Staring into her eyes, a flood of memories score through me. The first time I saw her beautiful, ginger laced curls blowing in the wind on the playground, I knew then I had never seen anything or anyone as beautiful. Recollections of the first time we kissed and carving our initials into a tree when she first agreed to be my girl shoot through my heart and straight to groin. Hardening like steel, I forge a little more of myself inside her opening, knowing with all certainty this was my wolf's plan all along. As much as I want to give all the credit to the copula for where we are right now, a deeper part of me knows this was always the plan.

Although we've been through heartbreak and to hell and back, knowing we found our way to one another gives me all the assurance I need to make love for the first time to my first love.

Planting a small kiss on her lips, I breathe deep into her mouth, inhaling her wholly. "I love you, Claudia Helsing."

Her eyes widen with surprise, but I don't give her a chance to respond when I slide deep into her depths. She gasps as I enter, and I feel her clench around my girth. Digging her nails into the small of my back, she lets out a curse as I inch deeper inside her. *This feels even better than the tip.*

"I love you Claudia Helsing," I repeat as I push the remainder of my leading into her pulsing center and she cries out in a flurry of ecstasy.

"Oh, Mark! I love you!" she exclaims, tugging my back, pushing me down on her. I feel her relax beneath me and she gyrates her hips, moving in rhythm with me.

In my entire life, I've never felt anything like this. So soft. So wet. So warm. So good. Tears well in the corner of my eyes and I cry out as her pulsing heat grips me like a vice.

Shit. I'm never coming out of her!

I don't know if it was my wolf or me, but finally we're in agreement.

Lifting up, I hold my hands at her sides as I pound in and out of her. Looking at her trusting, endearing gaze makes me want to be the man—no, the alpha she deserves. She deserves protection and all the love I can give her. And I plan to give her both. All day. Every day.

"You feel so good," she moans, meeting my thrusts.

Watching her big bouncy breasts is hypnotic. Surrendering to their lure, I pull one to my mouth, teasing her nipple with my tongue. Every part of her tastes so good.

Thrusting in and out of her, I alternate between slow and swift. I'm watchful of her expression as her eyes alone tell me what she likes more. As much as I want to be gentle, she seems to delight in a hard and fast pace.

Before I have a chance to change our position, I feel my muscles tense beneath my skin.

My wolf is awakened.

Growling, a deep, throaty snarl hurls through me and my pace quickens. Emitting a loud roar, my eyes flash, but when I see her eyes mirror my own, I know the mating is officially taking place. Her hold on me strengthens and she lifts her hips to meet my thrusts.

You will always feel protected. You will always be loved.

I hear my wolf's voice just as clear as if it were my own.

And so does she.

Claudia's eyes gush with tears and she pulls my face to hers and kisses me. But this kiss is different. Almost violent. Possessive. If I didn't know better, I'd think she was marking me. Perhaps an alpha spirit dwells deep within her already. Not surprising, she was meant for this.

Rubbing our noses together, I mark my scent on her.

Taking her hands, I guide them above her head.

"I'm about to imprint on you, beautiful. You're mine now."

"Mark, I've always been yours."

Her words alone almost make me cum. "Damn, you are perfect."

Once again, my muscles constrict and contort. It feels like I'm about to shift, but this is different. Although I've never done this before, I am finally trusting my wolf.

A bright, shimmering dew erupts from my pores, covering Claudia completely. As the dewy mist covers her body, she writhes tantalized by the touch upon her skin.

Roaring aloud once more, my thrusts become more brutal, and I feel my wolf taking over. Even more, I feel my leading enlarge, expanding within her as I watch her eyes gape open. Her sexy mouth cracks and I think about how lovely Claudia will look when I fill her mouth with other parts of me.

Without warning, I slide out of her and flip her on her knees.

Whimpering, she does as my wolf directs while I slap my leading against her opening, snarling when I see the tint of pink covering my shaft. While I don't count her virginity as some mere prize to be won, my wolf is emboldened at the sight of it. Knowing he is the first and only sends him into overdrive.

Forging my way back inside her once more, I am delighted to finally have her round ass on display. Soft and jiggling just for me. If the sight of the prettiest pearl I've ever seen, stretching open just for me wasn't enough, the wet sounds coming from her center as I drive in and out of her makes me feel like a fucking king. And this sweet pearl is my castle.

"King Me!" I roar, slapping her bottom and watching it shake just for me as I slam into her.

Panting, she meets my thrusts, ramming her butt hard against me. "You already are my king, baby!" she groans in response. "You rule my realms, Mark!"

"And you rule my heart, corazón!" I feel everything. The tightness of her pulsing center. Her dripping arousal. Her thick and soft walls. I can't imagine anything feeling as good as Claudia Helsing. "I'm giving you all of me. My name. My cum. My heart. It's yours, Lady Helsing!"

She grunts, arching her back, and looking over her shoulder at me. "Ahh… Mark! I love you!"

I'm riding the edge of my release. But I need to see her. Look her in the eyes when I fill her with all of me.

Pulling out of her once more, I flip her over and admire this perfect woman. Hair like fire, a heart of gold, and the prettiest pearl my eyes ever did see! Goodness knows I can't look at it without wanting to sink deep into her center. How I'll ever want to do anything but live inside of my mate, I'll never know.

"I need you to look at me when I cum inside you for the first time. I'm planting my seed deep in this pretty thing and then I'm gonna fuck you some more. Now open wide and show me what's mine."

Claudia has never looked happier than she does in this moment. Who knew all these years she only needed a good pounding to officially plaster a smile on that pretty face?

Lifting her legs, she crosses them like scissors, and then spreads them insanely far apart, showcasing my sweet treasure.

Impatient, I dip down inside her and my heart jolts when I feel her soaking hole wrap around my shaft. I'll never tire of this sweet thing right here.

A possessive snarl rips through me and I growl, slamming in and out of her. "Keep your legs high! Toes pointed!" I growl.

Claudia does as I instruct and the sight of her outstretched before me, drives me wild.

"You're gonna let me in here whenever. I'll need this sweetness every day!" I hear my wolf's words rip through me and Claudia shudders in my grip. I kiss her nipples, continuing my grind as I feel my release building.

"Whenever you want," she cries aloud, raking her fingers through my hair. "It's yours, baby!"

"And all of me is yours, mi amor," I croon into another kiss.

One final thrust and it feels like I'm holding a fire hose. Spraying the entirety of my seed into her, I have no doubt her belly will be round with my child or children in no time. The thought revs me up and I pound harder, exploding deeper into her depths.

Over the years I've released in my own hands more times than I can count. Now I know this is how it was always meant to be. Forged deep in my mate's sweet and tight hole, The sweetest place on earth.

Chapter 22

"Mark, you are such a liar!" Claudia laughs as she glides her hands along my chest.

I'm still working to catch my breath, but I give her a puzzled stare. "What are you talking about, beautiful?"

She giggles again, raking her tiny fingers against the hairs on my chest. "There's no way you're a virgin!"

Resting my head back into the pillow, I laugh. "Well, not anymore."

Kissing my chest, her fingers glide up to my chin and she tugs my beard so that I am looking at her. "I guess that goes for both of us." She casts a wicked smile and pulls me in for a kiss.

Once more, Claudia's kiss is just as possessive and assaulting as before. And I love it. I feel claimed. Owned. It's like she wants me to know she has sole authority over my lips. That's fine with me because she does.

As her mouth moves along the ravine of my neck and back to my chest, I instantly feel myself harden. It hasn't been ten minutes and my leading is already ravenous for more of her. With Claudia's leg propped between my thighs I know she feels the hardness there as it juts against her thigh.

Taking my length in her hands, she strums the tip, circling

her finger as she grips my girth.

"Mmm… I want more," she hums into my ear. "It's so big, baby, but I want it."

"You can take it all," I moan back, running my hands through her beautifully tousled mane.

Pushing my shoulders back, Claudia holds me steady as she straddles my waist, lining my leading up to her already slick center.

"Do you think I can get this monster in me," she giggles, rocking back and forth on my crown.

Gripping her hips, I grunt. Her teasing my tip is making me restless. "There's only one way to find out," I say, pushing her hips down.

"Ahh…" she moans as I expand the entirety of her. "Oh, it hurts baby." Her eyes are shut tight as she bites her lower lip. "But it feels so damn good."

Moving one hand up and along her waist, I take one of her breasts in my hand. Pressing against her nipple, I tease it, knowing she enjoys my touch. She wiggles some more against me, and I feel her wet center throbbing as I use my other hand to push her down some more.

"It's okay, beautiful. It may hurt now, but I promise it will feel so much better in a minute. Do you trust me?"

Her eyes open wide, once more beaming with hopefulness. "Yes, Mark, I trust you with all of me."

Affirming with my eyes only, I push my hips up, filling her with more of me. She winces as I do, crying out as I forge my way up into her depths. Finally her bottom lands along my thighs as the entirety of me plunges inside her and she screams a lilting cry.

Bouncing up and down, her breasts once again hypnotize

me, and I see nothing else but the perfection of the angel having her way on me.

"That's it baby! Have your way! Ride me hard!"

And that she does.

Arching her back, her wild tresses fly against her face, accenting her high cheekbones and her alluring frame. Willful grunts stir through her as she grinds deep, gripping my length along her slick folds.

Watching her large breasts bounce just for me is just as mesmerizing now as it's been eyeing her perfect rack over the last few days. I can't believe someone as beautiful as Claudia would ever feel insecure about herself. She is perfect in my eyes, and she always has been.

Firming my hold on her round bottom as it slaps against my thighs, I am thankful for every perfected inch of her curves and voluminous frame. Her soft tummy and thick hips assure me I'm making love to a beautiful grown woman. She's more than the girl I fell in love with all those years ago. She's my mate.

Taking both of her breasts in my hands, I work her nipples and am rewarded by a seeping gush of her wetness down my thigh. Lifting my head, I lick her nipples, then bring her breast to my mouth.

"Oh Mark! That feels so good." She whines, rocking her hips back and forth. "Don't stop!"

I am glad she lets me know what she likes. It gives me the confidence to keep going. This is all so new for me. I just want to please her and make her feel loved with every stroke of my hand and kiss of my lips.

Swirling her hips, Claudia cries out as her pulsing center grips me hard. She's on the edge of her orgasm and it's my job to see her through to the end.

"That's it baby. Keep going. You need to feel sweet and filthy. Let your sweet tide wash over me. I've got you."

And let it go she does. Screaming my name, she bucks hard, riding me like a jockey. But she's not the only one. I thought this one was all for her, but with the way her thick, soft center grips me, I'm forced to flood her gates with more of me.

Again, I feel my eyes well with tears as the ecstasy of this moment overtakes me. I want to cry like a baby, it feels that good. But I rein in my tears like the king she deserves. Strong. Defiant.

Instead, I meet her thrusts, holding her steady as I ram myself hard inside her with an unrelenting drive that makes her eyes fall to the back of her head.

This moment is priceless. I could look at her like this forever. With a hazy glare, an arched back, glowing with a sweaty sheen as she sits on top of me, it makes waiting all those years worth it.

I waited because I always wanted something better than what I saw when I was a kid. My parents didn't love each other. I promised myself I'd wait for a woman who loved me and wanted only me. There was a time I thought it was Claudia and then there was a time I thought that couldn't be further from the truth.

I am glad to say, I was right all along.

Chapter 23

The warm water pours down on both of us as we stand together in the shower. We were such a beautiful, sticky mess.

Since Claudia never finished her shower from before and I never got in with her as I planned, we thought this was a good time. Besides, she was still afraid the spider would return so she refused to come in here without me.

Holding me tight at my waist, Claudia nestles into my chest.

"It's okay, Claudia. No spiders," I smile, kissing her forehead.

"Are you sure?" She hugs me tighter, looking around the bathroom.

I kiss her once more. "I promise. Now come on, let's wash up and then get back to bed."

"But if we go back to bed, we'll just get messy all over again," she chuckles.

Laughing with her, I grab a small bottle of shampoo. "I suppose you have a point. But at least I can wash your hair for you."

Claudia frowns, puzzled. "Oh? You don't have to do that. It's such a tangled mess."

She reaches for the shampoo, but I pull back my hand. "But it's *my* tangled mess."

"Oh!" She gasps with wide eyes and her mouth stays parted. "Now turn around."

Claudia turns her back toward me. Her butt nestles firm against my already stiffening length and she leans her head back onto my shoulder.

"That's my good girl," I whisper, planting a kiss on her cheek. "You have to learn to let me take care of you. That's my job now. Do you understand?"

"Yes," she moans as I begin working the soapy lather in her hair.

"You have me now, beautiful. I'll always care for you. I'll always make sure you feel safe and loved." I kiss her again. "Growing up you always had to be the strong one. Take care of yourself. But you're not alone anymore, Claudia. Not only do you have me, but you'll have the protection of the Guard and this entire city to keep you safe."

Even with the water beating on her face, I still see a few tearful streams run along her jaw. I want to wipe away every tear from her eye. I need her to know she'll always be safe with me.

"Thank you, Mark," she cries. "You always looked out for me when we were kids. When we were apart, I felt so alone."

Turning her to face me, I plant a soft kiss on her lips. "You'll never be alone again, Lady Helsing. I promise you."

Throwing her head back, the water cascades down her back as the shampoo rinses from her hair. She's never looked more beautiful.

With her back arched, her perky rack beams bright as the water pours down her body.

I am one lucky man!

Smiling at me as she grabs the soap and a sponge, she presses her body to mine. "My turn."

As she rubs the soapy sponge against my body, I can't help moaning at the pleasurable feel. Washing my chest, shoulders, and arms, she hums a sweet melody as she scrubs me, lulling me into a peace I've never known before.

"That feels so good," I groan as I feel her breasts graze my chest and stomach as she washes me.

Moving to my hips, she circles around to my thighs and then stops.

"What's wrong?" I ask, and she casts me a sexy smirk.

Biting her lips, she looks up at me through her wet lashes. "Nothing. It's just nothing touches this, except me from now on. Not even a sponge." Gripping my manhood, her hands firm their hold along my shaft. "In fact, I think I'll take care of this myself."

Kneeling before me, she grabs my leading, using both of her hands. Taking the tip to her mouth, she kisses it, moaning as she does. A part of me wants to protest. I don't want her to feel like she has to do this. But I want her to do it. In fact, I need her to.

"Claudia," I drag her name out. "No one has ever—"

"And no one else ever will," she adds, taking the entirety of me into her sweet mouth.

A ragged breath is all I have as she overwhelms me with the depths of her throat. I doubt my mate has a gag reflex with the way she is taking me.

So sweet. So filthy.

Looking up at me, her lovely green eyes flash to gold and I now know with all certainty the imprinting took. She is my mate in every way. Seeing just a semblance of wolfen eyes resting in hers sends me in overdrive.

Firming my grasp in her hair, I gently nudge her forward. I want to see just how far she can go. And my baby meets my challenge more than I expected. Still, I don't want to unleash in her mouth. The only place my seed belongs is nestled in her sweet spot.

Lapping her tongue along my ridges, she hums again, and the tantalizing melodic tremors as her mouth wraps my shaft have me buzzing inside.

This is indeed a love song. One made just for me.

Still, I don't know how much more I can take before I explode. "Okay, baby come up for air. I'm not going to cum in your mouth."

Kissing my length once more, she looks up at me and smiles. "How did I do?"

"You are perfect," I say, pulling her up. "But we're far from done."

A low growl rumbles through me, and I lift her leg over my hip, straddling my waist. Pushing Claudia against the wall, I forge my way back inside her. It's not as easy as they make it look in movies. I'm sure the soapy water isn't helping either, but I don't care. I take hold of the grab bar at my side and use it as leverage as I work myself deeper inside.

Palming my face, Claudia caresses my beard, tugging it as she does. She pulls me into a kiss and firms her hold on my butt. Just that little amount of support helps me drive the remainder of my length into her depths.

Claudia gasps as I do, and I know I'm hitting her spot. "Right there!" She moans, gripping me hard.

It doesn't take long before we're both crying out as we reach our shared peaks.

I am totally enraptured by Claudia, engulfed in the entirety of her. Not only do I never want to let her out of my arms, but I also never want to leave the one place that I only hoped to find.

Her heart.

Chapter 24

Now this is a sight I could get used to. My naked mate standing in the doorway, holding a tray of strawberries. And with the way her sweet smile grips my heart, I know there's nothing I wouldn't do for her.

"Eres tan bella!" I groan in Spanish.

Shaking her head, a bashful smile crosses her face. "Now, Mark, you know I never learned Spanish. But it's good to see you still speak it." Placing the tray on the bed, she crawls beside me.

"Well, speaking it helps me keep a piece of my mother with me."

Resting her head on my chest, she nestles close. "That's good for you. I should've learned French so I could do the same for my mom. I mean I know a little, but it's mostly NOLA French so it's not quite the same. Goodness knows my father didn't pass down any real Irish traditions, so learning French would've been nice."

I wrap my arm around her, kissing her forehead. "You could always learn it. I'm sure either Dranoel or Cal would be happy to teach you. You know they are from Sierra Leone. They speak French all the time. It would be nice knowing if they're talking about me." I laugh.

"Oh, so you want me to be your spy?" She giggles.

Narrowing my eyes and adding a playful smirk. "My most trusted spy," I tease.

We both laugh but Claudia's eyes grow distant and her smile fades.

"Claudia? Baby, what are you thinking about?"

"I was just thinking about our mothers. I remember your mom. She was nice—you know the few times I met her when we were young. I remember how pretty she was with that wavy, long black hair."

"Yeah, she was beautiful. I only visited her once after she left us and returned to her home in Todos Santos. But the entire time I was there she refused to speak to me in English. She insisted I learn Spanish. Even when she wrote me letters, they were all in Spanish. My mother told me it was important I embraced all parts of me. My father's Scandinavian side and her Latin side. I didn't understand it when I was young, but I appreciate it now. Last year, I visited my abuela in Mexico. It was good seeing my family. Wolves there are different though. Everything is sacred. Everything has meaning. But family, is the most important. Ever since my trip, I knew that having a family was what I wanted."

"And you wanted that with Braelyn?" Claudia's voice is quiet, but I can tell it pains her to ask.

Yet, for the first time, it doesn't hurt me to hear it.

Lifting her chin to meet my eyes, I smile as I stare into her glassy glare.

"Well yes, I thought Braelyn and I had a future."

She swallows hard and dips her head, but I lift it back up.

"I guess what I'm saying is I learned everything, and everyone has a purpose. My mother once told me it was her duty as a Dunes wolf to secure the lineage of our kind. She said having me was her duty to protect our future. I didn't understand that then, but I do now. No, she didn't love my dad. And that bastard certainly didn't love her. But she said she believed my birth had a purpose and that one day I would come to know it. When I first stepped up as alpha, it was crucial that I had someone to ensure my bloodline. At the time Braelyn and I were together, so I thought naturally it was her. What happened, however, is my stepping up ensured my pack was finally free of the Dunes curse. Because of Braelyn my kin are no longer bound to its curse. But now, it will be our love, Claudia, that ensures we endure. Everyone has a role to play. Braelyn lived and loved me. I have to believe she fulfilled her purpose on this earth. But yours is just beginning mi amor. And your place is here at my side."

A steady stream of tears cascade down Claudia's face and she leans into my hold.

"You love me that much?" She cries, using her wrist to wipe her face.

"You bet I do," I say, tapping her nose, and pressing my forehead to hers.

Looking up at the ceiling, more tears race to Claudia's chin. "Thank you, Brae!"

Hugging Claudia tight, my eyes are now glassy pools of their own. This time I don't stifle their release. "Thank you, Braelyn!" I whisper, looking up. "Thank you."

Chapter 25

This is paradise.

Holding Claudia in my arms gives me a peace I didn't know I needed. For the last few weeks I've grieved, been angry, and riddled with guilt. Never did I think peace would be my portion. Even more, I never imagined in a thousand years that having Claudia in my life would be the reason for such serenity.

Not long after we offered a shared lament to Braelyn, for giving her life to even make this possible, did we find our bodies tethered together in a way only bound by love.

We made love for hours.

Literally a whole day. Besides eating and resting, we spent an entire day making sweet love.

But this time was different.

It was more than two people fulfilling carnal needs.

We did more than gyrate our hips. We made music. Using our bodies as instruments, we composed a sonata of our own. What we orchestrated was a melody so harmonious and so pure, there's no composer capable of scoring our love song.

Because we are in our own key signature.

We speak each other's language. We always have.

When we were young, everyone thought of me as the

playboy and Claudia, the heartbreaker. Sure, we both played the shallow part. But it's evident, neither of us want to play those roles anymore. We've grown. And now it's time for us to grow together.

Now, as I lay holding my lovebird in my arms, nothing but a heart of thankfulness rests within me.

Watching her sleep is my new favorite pastime. Even listening to her sounds that are somewhere in between humming and snoring, bring me joy. Although, I'm sure it's the way she curls into me, hugging my waist like she's afraid I'll go somewhere, making my heart leap.

Sunrise is almost upon us, and I want to wake Claudia up so we can see it together, but she's sleeping so sweetly, I don't want to disturb her. Besides, with the way we went at it for hours on end, I'm sure she needs all the rest to recover.

Me, on the other hand, I feel like a brand-new man. I could run twenty miles on just my two legs and not break a sweat.

Firming my hold on Claudia, a fresh scent like the smell of fresh cut flowers implodes my senses. The fragrant smell thickens, and an iridescent fog like the one covering our view of the den when we first arrived grows dense like smoke.

While no inner-alarm bells ring inside me, I can't help worrying if there is danger looming about. Thoughts of the gangly creatures from the other day stir a dreadful feeling inside me, and I go into protective mode.

"Claudia," I say, tapping her shoulder.

She grumbles something inaudible and plants her face into my chest.

Once more, I say her name, this time shaking her harder, hopeful she'll wake. As I do, the bed rattles.

What the fu— I didn't shake her that hard.

Jumping up, Claudia gazes around the room, bewildered. "Damn, baby! I was getting up!" Pouting her lips with the cutest protest, she gazes at me through her messy mane.

"That wasn't me." I answer, narrowing my eyes trying to see through the thick fog.

"Come on Mark, the sun isn't even up yet. Let me sleep a little longer," she whines, tossing her head onto her pillow.

Again, the bed shakes, but this time something is different. It's not just the bed, it's the entire house.

Pulling the pillow over her face she growls. "Mark!"

As much as I want to be impressed how the cadence of her growl so closely resembles mine, I don't have time. I need to understand what is going on.

Tugging the pillow from her face, and pushing her shoulder, I growl back. "Claudia, get up, beautiful."

She does as I ask, but when the den shakes again, she grips my bicep, leaning into my arm. "Mark, baby what's going on?"

Kissing her forehead, I turn so that I can get out of the bed. "That's what we need to find out."

Quickly throwing my shorts on, I walk to the doorway and peek around. Claudia jumps up, tossing her cloak on, she hovers behind me.

"Mark, what is it?" she whispers as the house shakes again.

This time the fog thickens into what looks like shiny snowflakes and a sweet floral scent permeates the air. The floor shakes beneath us and Claudia wraps her arms around my waist. I pull her into my hold, as I keep a watchful eye on the foggy mist.

A shimmering light breaks through every porthole window and beneath the crevice of the front door and a loud sound reminiscent of fireworks crackles in the dewy mist.

Slowly, the mist recedes, and my mouth falls open at the sight before us.

"Bless the Moon!" I gasp, taking a step into the main room. "I can't believe it."

Claudia maintains a tight hold at my back, keeping her face buried between my shoulder blades.

"What is it, Mark?" she grumbles, fearfully into my back.

"It's okay, baby. Take a look," I say, guiding her to my side. "I never thought I'd see the day."

Fretful, Claudia peers through her hands as they cover her face. Bit by bit, she allows her fingers to fall from shielding her view. Her mouth drops open and she turns to look up at me and then back again.

Throwing her hands to her mouth, her eyes grow wide. "Okay, Mark what just happened? Did we die or something? Is this heaven? What in the world!"

Looking up, I smile, shaking my head in disbelief. "No baby, we're not dead. Far from it. I only heard legends about this when I was a kid, but I never thought it was true."

Gazing around the den, gone are the dusty shutters and run-down interior. Instead, the room is brightened with fresh colors as if someone just painted. Even the dusty rocking chairs and sofa seem to return to former glory. The kitchen glistens and smells of fresh pine. Looking up, I smile noticing my tacky patchwork is no longer needed as the hole in the roof is gone. Claudia waves her hands around as we notice the wood paneling no longer reeks of decayed wood and the oak floors have regained their luster.

"How is any of this possible?" Claudia asks, tugging on my arm.

"When I was young, my mother told me legends of the

Primes. She said how they were capable of restoring beauty to world. But I never imagined anything like this."

Claudia's eyes scan the room in amazement. "Wow!"

"The last time I saw my abuela she said the reason she sent my mother to the copula ritual with my father was because her uncle, who was a brujo, predicted the rise of the Beta Primes would come from her bloodline. With my mother being her only child, she thought if the oracle came true this would be her only opportunity. But when it didn't the family began to lose hope. My grandmother never gave up. She told me, *'Nieto eres especial.'* Basically, she said, 'Grandson, you are special.' I just thought that was something grandparents are supposed to say."

Turning my face to her, Claudia's eyes well with tears and she tugs my beard and lifts to the balls of her feet and kisses my cheek. "You are special, Mark. If you didn't know it before, I hope you see it now."

"No, mi amor," I smile, planting a small kiss on her forehead. "We did this."

"What? I'm no wolf, Mark. This is obviously a Prime wolf thing."

Laughing, I wrap my arm around her. "Well yes, but this is a result of the copula, baby. I grew up hearing legends of mated primes whose love was so pure, so powerful, it brought beauty to all around it. That's why mating is important to wolves. Without it—without love we turn into the decrepit, cursed Skull wolves. But for alphas it's a necessity. And for Prime Alphas and Betas finding such a love is capable of thwarting even the gates of hell. I've found such a love, Claudia. I'm looking at her."

Another misty dew shimmers throughout the room and

I pull Claudia's mouth to mine. This time, the sparkling iridescence showers us as our lips lock as one. Tantalizing droplets fall on our skin, fusing a fervor of passion between us.

Before I know it, both my shorts and her cloak are on the floor. Lifting Claudia, she wraps her legs around my waist and once more I find myself inside her. A fervency so strong overtakes us as we make love and Claudia releases a howl that reaches not only the spirit of my wolf.

It reaches my heart.

Chapter 26

"Ahh, Mark!" Claudia screams. "Baby!"

I know she wants me to let her go, but I refuse. Not until I get everything I want.

Gripping her butt and with a tight hold on her waist, I keep her in place. I'm far from finished.

Once more, she lets out a shout and I keep working my tongue against her sweet spot. She may have been nervous as I was to try this, but I'm sure I'll never tire of this. Having her sweetness spread across my face as she rides my mouth has me devouring her depths in a way I never knew were possible.

"Mark, baby!" she cries out and I feel her throbbing center pulse along my tongue. Claudia's sweet nectar floods my face, dripping to my beard and it's the best thing I've ever tasted. Her orgasm continues as a tidal wave of passion rips through her, and I let her have her way.

She's all but spent when I lift her from my face, and I can tell she wants to rest. But she's not getting any. I need more. Her eyes widen in shock as I bring her hips to my ready and waiting leading, guiding her down my shaft. Already wet, she receives the entirety of me into her depths, crying out as she slides down on me.

"That's right baby, your alpha needs you to go for one more

ride," I grunt as the pleasurable feel of my girth expanding within her makes me desirous for all she has.

Her hooded glare as she rides me is the sexiest thing ever. She licks her lips and takes my hands in hers, moving them to her breast. Flicking her nipples with my tongue, I pull her close to me and push myself deeper inside her tight hole.

Pushing us up on the sofa so that I'm seated, I keep her legs straddled around my waist. I'm on the edge of not only the sofa, but my climax when she bucks faster along my length. Her big, bouncy breasts rake against my chest and it's the catalyst I need to release inside my beloved.

Growling hard, I unload everything I have into Claudia. With one more thrust, she ripples with an aftershock of her own as her head falls to my shoulder. Wrapping her into my embrace, I lean back into the sofa and try to catch my breath.

Looking around, I'm still amazed by the transformation.

I've always heard how Primes were the key to restoring beauty to the world but serving as a sort of second-class to the Altrinions, I never saw how such a thing was possible. But now that I've witnessed it for myself, I want for nothing than to see such a transformation in my city.

"It's time, baby," I say, pulling Claudia's hair to the side and kissing her cheek.

She sits up, staring at me slightly puzzled. "Baby, I know you said wolf mating is intense, but I don't know if I can take any more of your super-sized wolf D right now." Tossing her head back on my shoulder, she sighs like she wants to go back to sleep.

I can't help letting out a hearty chuckle. "Super-sized wolf D?" I laugh again.

She giggles, running her hand along my arms. "Well, what

else should I call that massive boulder you keep pounding inside me?"

"You can call it whatever you want, baby. It's yours," I say, and I feel new vigor ignite my manhood.

Claudia sits up. "Oh I know it's mine, but don't you think we should take a breather?"

Squeezing her butt, I grunt. "Well, all of this is mine now, Claudia Helsing. And just so we're clear, I plan on taking it whenever the hell I want." My eyes flash to their golden hue and hers widen. When my leading juts against her opening, her mouth parts. Placing my finger on her lips, I smile. "Don't worry, beautiful, the same applies for you. I'm here whenever you want me."

The tip of my leading forges inside her depths and she moans, letting her eyes fall back. "Baby," she moans. "I'm yours."

Wrapping her arm around my neck, she lifts up and then slides back down on me.

"Shit, baby, I wasn't even gonna ask to fuck again," I groan.

Grinding into me, she cries out and pulls my face to hers for a kiss. "I think they have a mind of their own," she breathes into our kiss. "Besides, you're always hard."

"Because you're always beautiful."

"And naked. Don't forget naked," she giggles as she bounces up and down. "Is that why you brought me out to your little cabin in the woods? So you can fuck me all day."

Thrusting in and out of her, I grip her hair hard. "Yeah, that's the plan," I growl, pulling her in for another kiss.

Claudia's hands trail my jawline, and she smiles. "I like that plan."

"So do I baby. So do I." I smile back.

Whatever I wanted to say earlier can wait.

Chapter 27

Once we finally pulled ourselves from yet another bout of passion, we realized it was well into the afternoon and we hadn't eaten. I made us some sandwiches while Claudia insisted on putting on her clothes. After making several jokes about me being some depraved wolf, luring her into my cabin for sex games, I threw her pants at her. I kidded it made more sense for her to be naked, because, if necessary, I'd just rip her clothes from her body and she'd be naked permanently.

The bottom line being, she'd be naked again. One way or the other.

It's been nice seeing the softer side of Claudia these last few days. This is how I remember her when we were kids. Once we broke up it seemed like all her walls went up. From there she became known as the stuck-up rich girl. I always hoped her softer side was still in there somewhere. I am glad I was right. She just needed the right person to bring it out.

Me, on the other hand, I'm thankful for Claudia not only helping me out of my grief but bringing a light back to my life I hadn't realized was gone. Just like this den, my heart was a hovel of despair after Braelyn's death. Actually, even before. Now there's a spring of hope welling within me, and I just want to shout it to the rooftops.

"Everything looks good! I'm famished!" Claudia says as she sits down at the table. "But baby, those are some colossal sandwiches."

"Look at me," I reply, gesturing my hand along my torso. "I'm six-three, two hundred and twenty-five pounds. I need to eat. This, my lady is your lunch." Offering her a small plate with a standard portion, she smiles, relieved.

"Well, thank the moon! I don't think I could scarf those down."

My heart thumps. Now she's speaking my lingo too? "So we're thanking the moon now?"

Her nose scrunches. "Oh did I say it wrong?"

"It's perfect, baby. Cute, is all." Leaning over, I kiss her forehead. I grab two bottles of water and put them on the table.

"Mmm… this is good! I haven't had muffuletta in forever! Not everyone can dress salami the way I like it."

Smirking, just the sight of her enjoying my food makes me happy. "I only aim to please, Lady Helsing."

Her eyes widen and she lets out a small cough. "Oh, about that," she starts, lifting a finger. Taking a quick swig of water, it seems like she's trying to get her words right. "So at first I thought you were just saying that in a moment of passion. But now—"

"Now what?" I take a bite of my sandwich, stuffing a few carrot sticks in my mouth. We don't have chips but I need something crunchy.

"I thought the notable, *Lady,* was only conferred once—"

"Once you take a place of notability. I think being the wife to an alpha—a prime alpha at that is rather notable. Don't you?" I shrug my shoulders and take another bite.

Claudia sits up in her chair and waves her hands at her sides. "Okay, Mark, don't mess with me! Are you saying what I think you're saying? Because if you're teasing me—"

"Oh I am pretty serious about making you my wife. I thought I said that before." My tone is nonchalant. Watching her squirm is actually enjoyable. I know I'm being an ass, but this is fun.

"Mark Avram Helsing!" she snaps, jumping up. "Now you said that when we were—um—"

"Fucking?" I laugh and push the remaining portion of my sandwich into my mouth.

Claudia's cheeks blush, but she bites her lip, refusing to give in. "Okay, okay!" She jumps up and down, once more waving her hands at her sides. "Mark! Be serious!"

"I am being serious," I laugh, wiping my mouth and leaning back into my chair. "But if you keep bouncing up and down like that, we may have to resume fu—"

"Mark!" She whines, leering over me.

Grabbing her waist, I pull her close. She stands in between my legs, and I take the time to just admire how stunning she is. I am so thankful this beautiful woman is all mine.

Taking her hand, I pull her to my lap. She sits on my knee, and I clasp our hands together. "Claudia, being with you the last few days has been amazing. We've laughed. We've loved. It's as though we never missed a beat. More than that, it's like together we caught up with the grown-up version of us. Just a few days ago, I was in a dark place. And somehow, and out of nowhere you brought me out of my darkness. I was fortunate enough to have you as my mate. Now, would you do me the honor and become my wife?

Claudia looks down and fidgets with her fingers. "Mark, I—"

"I love you, Claudia. I want to spend every waking minute as your husband. I promise to protect you always. I protect what I love—"

"Because I love to protect." Finishing the wolfen pledge, she smiles as teary streams run down her face. "Yes, Mark. Yes!"

Tossing her hands around my neck, she dives deep into my embrace. I feel her tears wet my neck and shoulders, and I kiss her cheek. Squeezing her tight, I inhale her scent. Vanilla and strawberries. Sweet and wild. And all mine.

"Are you sure about this?" Claudia quietly asks, pulling from my hold.

"Do you remember when I carved our initials in that tree at Jean Lafitte Park?" Claudia nods with a curious smile. "Do you also remember I said that one day you'd be my wife?"

Claudia laughs. "Mark, we were kids!" She pushes my shoulder and wipes her face.

"We were sixteen. Almost seventeen if I recall. But the point still remains, I knew then I wanted to make you my wife. Sure, we spent years apart, but this—this right here was always meant to be. I want more out of you than just a mate to bear my bloodline. I want—no I need—you to be my wife. My partner in life. Someone who will keep the light on for me when all the world around me is dark."

Claudia leans her forehead to mine and smiles. "I promise to always keep the lights on, baby."

Sitting back, I want to savor this moment, but then I remember what I wanted to say to her earlier.

"Thank you, beautiful. I'm gonna need it. Listen, while I want to sit here and bask in the details of getting you to the altar, we need to talk about something."

She swallows hard, kisses my forehead, and stands up. Patting her sides, she hooks her fingers in her pockets and paces the floor. "Okay, that's good, because there's something I wanted to talk to you about too."

"Me first—"

"But Mark, this is kind of important."

Standing from the table, I grab her wrist. "Yes, I'm sure it is and I'll be happy to hear it. But this is important. Look, I never got to tell you about what happened while I was out on my run the other day."

Her face falls for a second, but she scrunches her nose and lifts her chin. I can tell something is bothering her. I want to know what it is, but I need to warn her about what I encountered.

"What happened, Mark?"

"I finally saw what's been plaguing our city. The rabid fiends everyone has warned me about. Two of them made it past the LaCroix twins and cornered me in the lot."

Covering her mouth, Claudia gasps. "Oh no! Please tell me they didn't hurt you or worse get their venom on you!"

"So you have seen them before?"

"Yes, I have. Mark, a lot happened while you were in Bessie's Tavern. I've only seen them a few times. Each time I've been fortunate not to get close. The Guardians and Lord Nashoba have done a great job at keeping them under control in your absence."

"That's just it, Claudia. I can no longer be absent. While I'm thankful for my Prime Alpha, it's not his job to protect this city. The purview of Louisiana falls to me. As much as I'd like for nothing more than stay here with you, beautiful, it's time for us to leave. I need to be out there with my pack. I need to lead my people."

"Our people," she quickly says, narrowing her eyes.

"Yes, Lady Helsing. Our people." I smile. It warms my heart seeing how she's already making her place at my side. "So you understand? We need to return and officially complete the ritual so I can get to my duties. Don't worry, baby, I will not let anything take precedence over what we share, but I have to step it up."

"I understand, Mark. As long as you know, I'll make myself available to help you. However you need me, I'm here." She leans into my chest once more, and I hold her tight. I could hold her like this forever.

Chapter 28

As much as I wanted to keep Claudia in my arms, I told her we needed to get going. In no time, we cleaned up the kitchen, bedroom and bathroom and packed our duffle. We didn't have much, but the den looks so nice now, we want to keep it that way.

"Perhaps we can come back here from time to time," I say, setting the duffle at the door.

"You think that's possible?"

"Sure why not?"

"Well, it seems like such a fairytale. You know like a once in a lifetime type of thing."

"I guess, but I hope being a Beta Prime has some perks. You know like a Prime Airbnb or something like that."

We both laugh, but Claudia seems distracted. Fidgeting with her fingers, she paces back and forth.

"Look, Mark what I wanted to say earlier. It's about my father."

"Your father? Oh my goodness, Claudia! I'm so sorry."

She casts a curious frown, tilting her head. "Huh?"

"I went on and on about my family and you've lost your father. I'm sorry I haven't expressed my condolences to you."

"Mark, please you of all people know my relationship with

my father was complicated at best."

"Sure, I know. Neither of us had the best role models as dads. Mine was a philandering, son of a Viking who thought people were good for nothing but conquering. But that doesn't mean it hurt any less when he died."

Claudia's eyes glass and she tightens her mouth. Folding her arms, she flits her eyes up to the ceiling, resisting her tears.

Making my way to her, I take her shoulders in my hands. "Were you able to give him a proper burial?"

Shaking her head, she bites her lip. "No, there wasn't a funeral. I don't even know where his body is. That's what I wanted to talk to you about. You know I was on the run after everything so—"

"Crap! Now I understand. You never had a chance to bury him. Listen, I'll see to it myself. I spent years apart from my mom, but I at least was able to be there for her funeral. And since she's buried in my family lot with my father, I can always visit. You need that, Claudia. A place to visit him."

Claudia dips her chin to her shoulder, allowing her wavy mane to cover her face. Gently grazing my hands through her hair, I see the stream of tears pouring down her face. Her bottom lip quivers a bit, while her wide eyes slowly trail up to mine. If I didn't know better, I'd think she was scared.

Kissing her forehead, I pull her into my embrace. "Listen, Claudia you're not alone in this. At least not anymore. You've got me now. Me, the Guard, and the whole of Louisiana, if need be, to see to your every need. That I promise you."

"All I need is you, Mark," she cries into my chest.

"You've got me, baby."

Wiping her eyes, she leans away from me, but I keep my hands firm on her waist. I'm not letting her go.

"It's just that it's more than burying my father, Mark. It's how he died. It's about that night at the mansion. There's more—"

Knock. Knock.

A loud thump slices through Claudia's words.

"Are you expecting someone?" she asks, casting me a wary glance.

Turning toward the door, my eyes narrow as a low growl churns through me. "No. I haven't had a chance to call Dranoel or the LaCroix brothers."

Once more, a loud thud bangs against my door. A part of me fears that perhaps it's another one of those fiends from earlier. But when I catch a familiar scent waft past my nose, my worry lessens.

"It's Jackson," I whisper.

Claudia's lips part, surprised. "What is he doing here?" She mouths.

"I don't know. Even though I was about to call, I thought we had at least another day."

Making my way toward the door, Claudia tugs my arm. "Mark, before you open the door, I need to tell you about—"

"It's okay, beautiful. I promise we'll finish our discussion. But I can't very well leave my Prime Alpha standing outside."

Claudia's shoulders slump a bit, but she forces a smile, nodding her head for me to get the door.

I hardly expect to see the big and wide smile planted on Jackson's face when I open the door, but it makes me happy, nonetheless. He says nothing but pulls me into a strong bear hug before I can offer a greeting.

Squeezing me hard, my Prime Alpha hits my back equally as hard, laughing as he does.

"My man!" Jackson exclaims, gripping my shoulder as he stands back, staring at me. "You know as much as I wanted to believe this would work, even I had my doubts. But looking at this place—at the two of you—I am convinced more than ever this was always meant to be." His chest puffs with pride as he looks on. Shifting his gaze from me and over my shoulder to Claudia as she stands just behind me, his broad smile stretches from ear to ear.

Smiling in return, I bow my head dutifully. "I couldn't agree more, my Lord."

Claudia mimics my motion and Jackson slides by us and enters the den. With his hands at his waist, he paces about, admiring the sight of it all.

"Absolutely amazing!" He says, almost breathless. "I mean truly this is stuff of legend!"

Claudia and I exchange glances and I know we're both thinking the same thing.

"My lord," Claudia begins. "I'm sorry but how did you know that we—um—"

Quickly, looking over my shoulder, I shake my head in warning. "Claudia!" I grit my words.

Lifting his hand in caution, Jackson smiles and chuckles once more. "It's quite all right, Lord Helsing. Your mate has every right to ask questions. She will be a part of our world after all, and she should know how things work. Having your mate know everything up front eliminates so many problems later. Trust me on this."

Jackson's eyes grow distant, and I know he's thinking about Damina, but he pushes the thought aside. Lifting to the balls of his feet, he folds his arms across his chest, clenching his jaw tight.

"Well, for starters, as a Prime Alpha, I am connected to every alpha. Even more so with a Beta Prime such as yourself, Lord Helsing. Your joy, sadness, and the full range of your emotions live on in me. I knew when you were ready. Not only that, but I could feel when the copula had taken root. It was like a thunderbolt burrowing deep in my bones. Quite frankly, it unlocked a part of me I never felt before. But as a Beta, you also unlocked an ancient gift. It's been centuries since a Prime wolf has garnered this transformative power during a copula ritual. The old ones used to say a Prime capable of such power could one day restore the balance of nature itself. Simply put, your future is indeed bright." Lingering a bit to ensure I grasped the weight of his words, Jackson's eyes once more flit to Claudia. "And for the record, I'm talking about both of you."

"My Lord!" I exclaim, dropping to my knee, with my fist over my heart. Claudia falls to her knee at my side, lowering her head in submission. I can't help but look over my shoulder at her and smile. I never thought I'd see a day when Claudia DeVeaux would even consider doing anything like this.

By and by, this woman reminds me just how much I've underestimated her over the years.

"Please," Jackson starts, gesturing his hand for us to rise. "Save the formalities for later. We have a few people waiting to greet you." Once more, Jackson's wide smile returns, and he extends his hands behind us toward the door.

Turning, both Claudia and I are surprised to find a small brood of wolves outside the door. Nothing but bright golden eyes and gleaming smiles meet us as we stare on in shock.

My heart leaps as the surprise of it all overtakes me.

Taking Claudia's hand in mine, I lead us outside. Never did

I ever think Claudia and I would find ourselves back together. Even more, I never expected to feel this whole, happy, and complete ever again.

I suppose that's why the old adage is true.

Never say never.

Chapter 29

Aclamoring chorus of shouts, whistles, and cheers greet us as we step outside. Looking out at over fifteen den leaders and at least five alphas from neighboring states assembled before us, my heart bubbles with joy.

With the sunset looming just above the tree line behind our supporters, I can say next to Claudia, I have never seen a sight as breathtaking.

Most of the familiar faces, Dranoel, Lorien, Cal, Dilano, Alana, and the LaCroix brothers stand out. Even some of the Lothian Den, like Kyra and Merle are here to my surprise. But there's one face missing.

Brian.

I want to ask Jackson where he is, but Jackson clears his throat, coming out of the den behind me and Claudia. Lifting his fist to quiet the crowd, he saunters to the middle of the lot.

"Today, you are witnessing history in the making! Not only has Lord Helsing, by assuming his role as Beta Prime, lifted the Dunes curse of the moon, but has brought back the ancient gifts to Beta Prime order!"

Once more, a series of cheerful claps surround us. Pulling Claudia closer to my side, she leans her head on my shoulder.

"Now through the commencement of the copula, Lord Helsing has both ensured his bloodline and retained your assurances never to be bound to the will of the moon again!" The crowd echoes Jackson's sentiment with a loud howl.

Howling in reply, I watch as the cadence of my yowl ignites the bright glow of the eyes of each alpha. The remaining den leaders roar back, dropping to their knees in submission.

I feel Claudia begin to lower herself as well, but I tug her arm tight, locking it with mine.

"It's okay, baby," I say, kissing her forehead. "We rise and fall together," I whisper in her ear.

"Together," she breathes back.

"Always," I smile, tightening the lock of our arms together.

By the mere wave of Jackson's hand, everyone lines up and makes their way toward us. Each one gestures a manner of either submission or acceptance as they pass by. While I'm happy to see everyone, not seeing Brian concerns me. He is supposed to be my second. My beta. Perhaps Jackson left him behind to look over things. Especially with those gangly creatures roaming about, it makes sense. Yet, it still feels odd not to have him here.

I can't help wondering if he still objects to me mating Claudia. Perhaps he chose to stay behind to avoid making this moment awkward. As much as the thought bothers me, it would be a wise choice for him to stay behind if his apathy for Claudia continues. I'd rather not have him sully the mood.

A few of the alphas and Dilano pull me aside, and I realize it's the first time Claudia and I have been an inch away from one another. Not since my last shift have Claudia and I been apart. We've been glued to one another since we made love.

Even though she's not more than two arm's lengths from me

now, just the thought of her being that far nearly drives me mad. I can hardly help looking away from my conversation with the alphas to her and Alana.

As much as I wish she was by my side right now, I am happy to see Claudia and Alana talking again. Claudia, Alana, and Dauphine were all as thick as thieves when we were teens. Alana and Dilano became a couple around the same time as me and Claudia broke up. Dilano naturally sided with me, and Alana fell in line. Dauphine maintained her duplicitous pretense, siding as Claudia's friend. If either of us knew then what we know now, we could have avoided so much heartache.

Perhaps even Braelyn would still be alive.

Although I don't discount the love we shared in our short time together, I'd trade it to know Braelyn was still alive. She gave up her life as a vampire to be with me. And while she may not fault me, a part of me will always feel responsible for her death.

But I suppose everything has a purpose.

"So like I was saying Mark, we're joining the circus soon. You know anything to feed the elephants," Dilano says with a chuckle.

"Yes, yes, that's important," I reply with my eyes still plastered to Claudia. The two share a hug and I can't help wondering what they're saying.

Shoving my shoulder, Dilano laughs again. "Earth to Lord Helsing!" he shouts and the alphas surrounding us join in a chorus of laughter.

"Huh?" I turn back toward everyone, confused.

"Ah, yes!" Merle, alpha of the Lothian Den, begins. "Lord Helsing has got those puppy dog eyes indeed! I know it well!"

The rest of the men continue poking fun and I do my best to

shrug it off. Watching the happiness spread across Claudia's face makes my heart leap.

"Let him alone!" Jackson adds, coming to our huddle. "That's exactly how the copula should work. There's no doubt this has been a good and fine mating for the happy couple!" With a sturdy pat to my back, Jackson and the others continue their laughter.

"I'm sorry I'm so distracted, my lord. It's just—"

Raising his palms in protest, Jackson shakes his head, still smiling wide. "No apologies needed young alpha. Not at all. However, I do want to discuss something of importance." Jackson's brows furrow and his lips draw into a thin line. It doesn't take a genius to know this is serious.

Allowing one more glance at Claudia, I feel at ease to see her and Alana laughing.

Doing my best to force my longing for my beloved aside, I straighten my posture. "Yes, my lord. How can I help?"

Gently squeezing my shoulder, he turns me so that my back is to Claudia. If it were anyone other than my Prime Alpha pulling my attention from Claudia, I'd shake them off. But seeing as how gracious Jackson has been toward me, I at least owe him my full attention.

"The LaCroix brothers informed Dranoel that you got your first look at the newest addition to the vile creatures of the night."

My eyes grow wide in alarm as I think on their gangly form. Just the thought of them so close to Claudia freaks me out.

"Yes, Lord Nashoba, there were two of them that made it just past the gates. What are those things? And how do they walk in daylight? Are they not some form of Scourge Vampire?"

"At first, we thought the same. We slaughtered over a dozen

on their first night about a week after Dacari's pronouncement over the Scourge. But when we found more on the morning after we realized these were something else. While they aren't as active in the daylight—they can yet attack in both the day and night."

"I'm so sorry, my lord. I've left you all to fight these things on your own."

Jackson's face relaxes into a smile. "You were grieving. Everyone has a right to mourn. Even alphas."

I want to ask him how he remains so stoic and strong despite it all, but rein in the thought. I'd rather not put it out there in front of the rest of the alphas. Although some of their eyes betray them. I'm sure they want to know how our Prime Alpha stays so grounded just as much as I do. But like most men, no one is interested in putting their feelings on the line.

"But Lord Nashoba," Dilano begins, concern filling between his thick, black brows. "Do we know how they came to be? I mean Dacari only lifted the scourged curse from the vampires. Right? I thought the whole point of her incantation was to ensure vampires not succumb to bloodlust, but rather exist more peacefully like their progenitors, Altrinion Vampires."

"That's just it, Dilano. Mortal made vampires don't have the capability to receive the power bestowed upon supernaturals like Altrinions. So the running theory is, when former Scourge—or mortal made vampires bite a human, that human becomes infected. Yet instead of turning into a vampire—they become more zombie like. Driven purely by an insatiable desire to feed."

Stepping forward just a bit, Joaquin, an alpha from Biloxi, lifts his forefinger. Shaking his head, he grumbles, "So what is being done to control these fiends? Many of the alphas and den leaders fear this madness will spread into other territories."

A few of the other alphas join in their shared complaint to Jackson. While he does his best to ease their worry, I can tell he's grown more than frustrated with their tone. Even though I haven't been around to see the impact of these creatures in the real world, everything in me wants to stay at my Prime Alpha's side, ensuring that alpha or not, everyone stays respectful.

But there's one thing pulling my attention.

Looking out among the crowd and not seeing Claudia.

Chapter 30

"Claudia!" I grit through my teeth, turning about. My eyes scan the entirety of the woods, but I don't see her. Peering past the tree line, I use my sharp vision and sense of body heat, but she's nowhere to be found.

Stepping back and away from the intense huddle forming around Jackson, I make my way to Alana.

"Hey Alana," I begin, trying to keep my tone cool. "Where's Claudia? I thought she was over here with you."

Alana shares her usually bright smile, but when she doesn't get the same in return, her smile fades. "Oh, I'm sorry Lord Helsing. She was just here a minute ago and then she was gone. I can look for her if you want."

"It's okay, Alana. I'll find her." My tone is more curt than I intend, but I don't take the time to apologize either. Before Alana can reply, I'm make my way to the middle of the courtyard, circling about. I wonder where she is.

Making a full three-sixty, my heart races as I wonder where she could be.

"Lord Helsing," I hear Lorien call my name as I press my way through the throngs of endearing wolves as I look around for Claudia. He's on my heel as I do, calling my name once more. Grabbing my arm, I turn quickly to see his lanky frame and awkward smile staring back at me.

I really don't have time for this. "Yes, Lorien, what is it?" I snap.

Lorien's shoulders jump a bit, but he forces his hands in his pockets and gazes at his feet. "Are you looking for your mate, my lord?" His voice sounds nervous, but his eyes flit over my shoulder.

I nod, drawing my mouth into a thin line, annoyed. "Have you seen her?"

"Yes, my lord, I saw her go into the den keep."

Lorien's words surprise me. I never saw Claudia go past me back inside. Still, knowing she's not lost—or worse, helps me more than he can possibly understand.

Heaving a sigh of relief, I hold myself at my waist, and firm my palm on his shoulder. "Ahh, thank you Lorien. For a minute there, I was getting worried." Squeezing his deltoid, I smile and turn around.

"My lord," Lorien continues, tugging my arm again, "but there might be some reason for worry, I'm afraid."

Snatching his jacket collar, I pull him close. "What do you mean?"

"Hey, what's going on here?" Dilano says, coming to my side. Carrying his gaze around the lot, I know Dilano worries what others may think.

Allowing my eyes a moment to roam about, I'm happy to see most are still enthralled in their conversations with Jackson. Only Alana, Dranoel, and the LaCroix brothers seem to notice what's happening here.

"Answer me!" I order, releasing his jacket.

Lorien flounders back a bit, and he flattens his palm against his torso and legs as though he were wiping the wrinkles away.

"She's not alone, my lord."

The worry in Lorien's eyes say it all. Claudia is in trouble. It doesn't take a genius to know something is wrong. I should've known Claudia wouldn't just walk off on her own.

I'm at the threshold of the den in a flash, fearing who could be with Claudia. My first thought is that Brian has somehow showed up. And while just the notion infuriates me, not catching Brian's scent when I enter troubles me.

There is another scent in the room. A scent I've never encountered before. It reeks of death and the most venomous poison.

But it's Claudia's frozen stance as I stare on at her back troubling me. I know there is someone else in the room, even though I can't see them beyond the shadows, I can sense their presence.

"Claudia?" I call her name, but she doesn't respond. Instead, she stands eerily still.

"Well, don't just stand there dearest. Since we're practically family, now is as perfect time as any for us to formally meet."

Although I've never met her before, hearing Chartreuse Grenoble's venomous voice from across the room, is just as bone chilling as the stories I've been told.

Treading carefully, I make my way to Claudia's side. Before I take a moment to give any reply to Chartreuse, I take a long hard stare at Claudia. I need to see her face. Make sure she isn't harmed. Slowly, Claudia turns her face to me and the tearful, pain-staked glare she gives me wrenches my gut in knots. Her eyes alone are apologetic, and I know whatever comes next won't be good.

Releasing a shrilling cackle, Chartreuse steps out of the shadows into the light. With one hand on her hip, she saunters slowly into the middle of the room. Even her movements seem threatening. As she places one long leg in front of the other, her high heeled boot barely makes a sound against the wood. Dressed impeccably, wearing black leather pants and a black lace shirt just the look of her is enough to turn anyone's head. But I know better.

Despite her upswept hair, that is strangely brighter than Claudia's red mane, and the soft features of her oval face, I know a killer lives beneath it all.

Chartreuse Grenoble has not only killed more of my kind than I care to count, but she also stalked and killed Damina's parents. She's renowned in the supernatural community for her villainy. Limericks of mulberry and juniper trees are synonymous with her name, as she's been known to sing songs to her prey before she kills them.

Knowing she and Claudia are kin hasn't always been an easy pill to swallow, but one thing I know for sure, Claudia is nothing like her wretched ancestor.

Wiping a few loose tears from Claudia's face, I cup her chin. "Are you okay, Claudia? Did she hurt you?"

Laughing once more, Chartreuse waves her hand dismissively before placing it over her chest. "Why dearest would you assume I'm the aggressor? I mean, I'm not the one with the dagger that sought to kill your beloved Jerrica Jeffers."

"What?" I breathe back.

Claudia's eyes fall as I cast my gaze between she and Chartreuse. More tears freefall to her chin and I slowly release her from my grip.

Shock rolls over me and my worst fears push out from the darkest corner of my mind. "Claudia?" I whisper, stepping back. "I thought you said—you told me—"

Cupping her mouth, Claudia lifts her free hand in protest. "Mark, I—I—"

"And I told you from the beginning that this woman can't be trusted. Now you know the truth!" Hearing Brian's grizzly tone hits me straight in my gut as I turn to see him now in the doorway.

Where did he come from?

Frozen, I remain still. I fear if I move, with the way I feel right now, anyone in this den would surely feel the brunt of my anger.

Turning my gaze back to Claudia, her tear-worn face does little to assuage my angst.

"Claudia, please tell me you didn't." I keep my gaze low, for fear just her sweet face alone forces me to let down my guard. I can't afford to do that this time around.

Parting her lips to speak, more tears gush from her eyes. "Mark, baby just let me explain."

"There's nothing left to say, Claudia DeVeaux!" Brian barks, walking to my side. "I knew you were bad news all along. But your relation to this leech paints the picture so clearly. Now it's no wonder you attacked Jerrica. Chartreuse has long hated her. But I will not stand here and let you do the same to Mark. No. Not on my watch!"

Claudia's face reddens at his words, and she bawls into her cupped hands. "Mark, I—I'm so sorry. I tried to tell you! If you'd just let me—"

"Oh tsk, tsk, poor girl," Chartreuse begins, slithering to Claudia's side. "You are of my blood, girl. And we never settle as pawns or allow the whim of men control our way." Chartreuse's bright eyes flash with a greenish hue as she regards me and Brian. Her fangs lengthen, but her expression softens as she turns back to Claudia. Placing her hand on Claudia's chin, she brings Claudia's eyes to hers. "Lift your head high, young one. No matter our reasons, our deeds of the dark require no consent from the likes of men. Hold your head high, my girl. Let them see there remains neither fear nor fret in your eyes." Slowly, Chartreuse's pointy black nail trails the etching of Claudia's jawline. Releasing another shrilling cackle, her darkened eyes gleam with the darkest pride as Claudia lifts her chin as she turns to me and Brian.

Squaring her posture as she stands shoulder to shoulder with Chartreuse, Claudia's eyes narrow. Looking at her, I am more than shocked at her resemblance to her wretched kin.

So much so, I almost don't recognize her.

Chapter 31

"That's it, young one," Chartreuse breathes into Claudia's neck. "Disavow regret. Steady your footing. Don't let them see you flinch. Not even for a minute." Casting a dark grin at us, Chartreuse is more than pleased.

A mischievous smirk crowds the corner of Claudia's mouth. Gone are the soft curves of her lips that drove me wild only hours ago. As her eyes darken as she sets her sights on me and Brian, I fear I gave myself to love's lure too quickly. Perhaps it wasn't love at all. Lust, possibly.

But I know what I felt.

I thought what we shared these last few days was real. But Brian was right. What else did I expect from Chartreuse's bloodline?

Dalcour has long warned us to stay clear of Chartreuse. According to her sire, her villainy was far beyond repair. Truer words have never been as clear as they are right now.

Before I have a moment to ponder Claudia's duplicity, the floor quakes at our feet, and the whole den keep rattles. A thick fog permeates the air and I feel my heart sink to the floor. Everything I thought to be real is slowly fading.

Looking around, I all but expect the den to return to the hovel it once became, but I am strangely surprised that our surroundings merely lose their luster, but the place remains intact.

Strange.

"I'm sorry, my lord," Brian begins, placing his hand on my shoulder. "But it's better the truth come out now."

Keeping my eyes on Claudia, I wish I could stop looking at her, but I cannot. While there's a part of me that sees her likeness to Chartreuse clearer than ever, I still can't help seeing a sliver of the woman I confessed my love to as I explored her depths. Surely what we shared or the love we made can't be a lie.

"I thought you loved me, Claudia. I thought we—together—bared our truth to one another. I thought what we had was real." My wispy words are barely audible, but I know she hears me. For a minute, I swear I see her posture soften, but she remains stoic.

"Aww, isn't that adorable?" Chartreuse shrieks, clapping her hands. "I mean when I sent you and Colin to kill Jerrica, I was rather miffed that she yet lived. But I see you're playing the long game, young one. All my years killing these brute mutts, and I never thought to seduce any. What better way to lessen their defenses than getting to the heart of it all? Going after the alpha. Splendid!" Screeching an earsplitting scream, Chartreuse claps her hands once more, before throwing her arm around Claudia's shoulder.

"You see, my lord," Brian says, circling me to catch my eyes, averting my gaze from Claudia. "She's been working with her this whole time!"

My heart plummets once more to my gut and it feels like the wind got knocked out of me. How could I be so stupid?

"What is she doing here?" I hear my Prime Alpha barge into

the den. Jackson quickly makes his way to my side. Tugging my arm and turning me toward him, he searches my face. His eyes are laden in alarm and it's taking everything in me to hold back both my anger and sadness.

One loose tear falls to my chin and Jackson's mouth draws to a thin line. His eyes fall and it's almost as if he's just as heartbroken as I am. No one else in this room wanted this to work more than he did.

"Ah, so you must be the Prime Alpha I've heard so much about!" Chartreuse exclaims, circling around Claudia. Stopping once more at Claudia's side, she props her arm on Claudia's shoulder. "So how's that pretty little mate of yours doing? Damina, is it? Oh, I hear she's chomping at the bit these days!" A calculating grin covers her face and I know she's hoping to get a rise out of Jackson.

Issuing only a low growl in reply, his eyes flash bright and even the floor rumbles beneath his feet.

"Oh you Prime wolves are full of all sorts of neat little parlor tricks!" Chartreuse laughs, while feigning a yawn and waving a dismissive hand.

"Just give me the word!" Brian grits his teeth, coming in between me and Jackson. Snarling, his chest heaves up and down as he leans forward, ready to lunge at Chartreuse and Claudia.

Still, the sight of Brian wanting to hurt Claudia pains me, and I grab his wrist, shaking my head in warning.

"But my lord? She's all but proven she's aligned herself with Grenoble! Just give the word and I—"

"And you'll do what?" Claudia snaps, finally speaking. Her anger is all but kindled as she regards Brian. "You've done nothing but threaten to end me since the copula commenced.

You'll not lay a finger on me! That, I promise you!"

Brian growls, crouching low, ready to pounce.

"Oh this is getting exciting!" Chartreuse claps, clasping her hand under her chin.

Once more, Brian snarls, and I see his muscles tense as though he wanted to shift.

"Stand down, Brian!" Jackson warns, as he keeps his sights on Chartreuse and Claudia.

"Let me loose!" Brian yells over his shoulder when he feels my hand tighten around his wrist.

"Brian, no!" I shout.

"Claudia," Jackson begins, stepping in front of Brian, "please tell us you've not aligned yourself with Chartreuse. Tell us you have nothing to do with her schemes." His voice is calmer than I expected, but Jackson never seems to allow much to rattle him.

Claudia's face softens as she regards Jackson, but she doesn't let it sit long. Sucking in a breath, she lifts her head again, narrowing her eyes with a daggered-eyed glare to match.

"For once, Claudia, just tell me the truth," I sigh. I just need to rip the bandage off.

"For once?" She echoes, tilting her head the way she does when she's annoyed. Her eyes well with tears and I can only wonder why my words surprise her.

"He deserves the truth, Claudia," Jackson adds, placing his hand on my shoulder.

Brian grabs my other shoulder and points at Claudia with his free hand. "And it's the truth you'll never get from this one! She knows nothing of truth."

"Sapphirus stone." Claudia's tone remains surprisingly calm. She's not the unnerved woman I scented when the ritual first began at Bessie's Tavern when she first asked for the stone. No, this woman is more sure of herself than before. Neither Brian's barking tone nor his insinuation of her guilt plague her this time around. Stepping forward, she sets her sights on Brian. "You want the truth? Give me the stone. I'll give you the truth." Extending her hand, she gestures for Brian to place the stone in her palm.

Grumbling, Brian remains still. He looks over his shoulder at me before casting his gaze to Jackson.

"Oh dearest!" Chartreuse cackles. "Cat got your tongue?" She and Claudia share a laugh. But it's the wicked smirk Claudia gives Chartreuse that worries me more. "So do you have the stone or not? Claudia here has nothing to hide. But oddly I don't sense the stone's power. So I suppose we'll never know."

"I'm sorry, my lords," Brian laments to me and Jackson. "I—I don't have it." Lowering his head, Brian steps behind me and Jackson.

"It's okay, Brian. I don't need a stone. I think the truth is plain before us now," I say. Once more the floor shakes beneath us and the mist thickens.

"No, my lord," Claudia whispers, her eyes glassy. "We're far from the truth. But I'll not let you leave without hearing the truth from me." Stepping forward, Claudia's eyes plead with me to hear her out.

"Ah-hem," a small faux cough from the doorway turns our attention.

My jaw drops in surprise as does Jackson's when we see Dacari Peyroux, Damina's cousin, standing at the threshold. Despite every ounce of melancholy in the den, Dacari jauntily saunters inside. Bouncing into the room with a bright smile I know is only intended for Brian, she gives him a quick wink. Her hard leather Doc Martins stomp against the wood floor as she strolls into the room. Bobbing her head over shoulder, her long braided locks swing against her back as she eyes the doorway. But it's the tall, broad, dark frame of Decaux Marchand stepping into the room that officially makes this place feel small and suffocating.

Slightly lifting his fedora, revealing his darkened crimson eyes, Decaux leans against the wall with his arms folded at his chest. "Well, I hope we're not too late. It looks like you already got this party started without us." Rubbing his hand against his stubble, he swirls his finger along the brim of his hat, blowing a kiss toward Chartreuse. "Fancy meeting you here, my little siren. Fancy meeting you here indeed."

Gasping, Chartreuse skulks backward, just beyond the shadows. Her eyes widen with both disbelief and surprise. And for the first time, I see fear in her eyes. Chartreuse may be evil. But Decaux is the devil.

"What are you doing here?" She hisses, with her arms pressed against the bedroom door.

Twirling a blue stone between his fingers, Decaux smirks. "Oh, isn't this just what you asked for, love?"

Chapter 32

Balancing the stone on the tip of his forefinger, Decaux's cagey grin stretches from ear to ear. His gaze lingers on Chartreuse and the trepidation his presence causes her gives me a glint of hope.

Even if that hope comes from the devil himself.

"Marchand!" Jackson shouts, breaking the darted-eye stare between Chartreuse and Decaux. "What are you doing here?"

Pushing himself from the wall, he chuckles and makes his way next to Dacari. "I would think a thank you would be in order here. I mean it took more than a little persuading for me to procure this stone. And it seems my timing impeccable if I don't say so myself." He sneers his words as the crimson embers of his Altrinion eyes glow bright.

"I asked him to come, my lord," Brian admits with his head lowered slightly.

"Why, B? Why would you go to Decaux of all people?" I mutter back. Although I know everyone in this room can hear me, even I am surprised by Brian's actions.

"How in the hell could you bring him on pack soil? You of all people know that neither vampires nor Altrinion vampires can come on pack soil uninvited. And such an invitation can only come from an alpha or a—"

"A tribrid?" Dacari smiles, waving around the room. "I mean I'm a wolf, a vampire, an Altrinion, you name it. Just like all things New Orleans, I'm just a little hot bowl of gumbo. Or jambalaya." Hunching her shoulders like it's no big deal, Dacari keeps her incredibly bright smile plastered on her face.

Looking at Brian as she speaks it's clear the woman has him in a tailspin. There's no doubt he's madly in love with her. He must be to bring her here. Despite how bad things are right now, I can't help still being happy for him.

While I can tell Brian wants to linger in his abandoned thoughts as he stares at his mate, he tightens his mouth, losing the boyish grin he's had since she arrived. "Because I refuse to allow you to be duped by any descendant of Chartreuse Grenoble! Isn't it evident, now more than ever we—no you need the truth? Besides, believe it or not he's on our side."

"Oh one thing I can assure you, is that Decaux Marchand is on no one's side, dear one," Chartreuse gripes from across the room. "In the Marchand book there's only one side. Marchand."

Laughing, Decaux rubs his chin. "Ha! You're one to talk, love. And I suppose had you said such a few months ago, I would wholeheartedly agree with you. But much has changed since we last spoke, Chartreuse. In fact, I think it would surprise you to know that I, the son of the devil himself, yet walks in the light. I am officially an Altrinion-vampire no longer bound to the curse of the sun."

"Impossible!" Chartreuse gasps in disbelief.

"Oh, it's quite possible, I'm afraid. Well, then again you may have missed some things whilst you've been scouring the earth wreaking havoc. By goodness, hasn't anyone told you? I'm a father now! This beauty here is my daughter, Dacari Peyroux.

Since I've become a father, I've finally found a love powerful enough to bring me out of the dark. Once and perhaps, for all." The cynicism in Decaux's tone is hard to miss. But the danger in his eyes even more so.

Everyone in the supernatural community has long known Chartreuse has vowed to end the Peyroux wolf bloodline since the day her lover Scotty was murdered by Dacari's ancestors over a century ago. From that time the Peyroux's have remained hidden. What's worse, Decaux knows of Chartreuse's vendetta. His mentioning of Dacari is no mere introduction. It is a warning.

Gulping, a defiant gleam brightens Chartreuse's eyes. Just as she said to Claudia, Chartreuse has no plans of quivering before any man. Even Decaux Marchand.

"It matters not!" Chartreuse contends. "I care nothing of stones or this haggard reunion of sorts. I came for one thing and one thing only. My blade."

"Your blade?" Jackson questions, confused. His eyes glance around and each of us seem just as baffled. Everyone except one person.

"Claudia?" I growl, inching close to Claudia. Brian holds my shoulder as he keeps his eyes on Chartreuse. Thankfully, Chartreuse seems more concerned with Decaux's arrival and pays little attention to either me or Brian. "Please don't tell me you have her blade? Not the same one you used to try to kill Jerrica!"

"I told you, my lord. It was probably her intent to kill you while you slept."

Releasing a growl of her own, Claudia's eyes flash bright. "That's not true!"

My heart thumps at the sight. How can my wolf imprint on

her, shift the essence of my power to someone who means me and my pack harm? I thought I could trust my wolf. It seems he's just as daft as me. Horny and stupid.

Even Chartreuse seems perplexed. Pouting, her puzzled gaze softens as she stares at Claudia. "Well, dear it's okay to admit the truth to me. I mean I know my blade is here. As even Decaux knows, my blade and I are bonded. I can track it no matter its location. For days it's been held up at that Tavern. The border that harpy Melvina keeps up, prevents me from entering. But just a few hours ago I detected it here, in this very lot. So just hand it over and I'll be on my way."

Clenching her eyes tight, Claudia's jaw tightens. Turning to Decaux, Claudia offers her hand. "The stone, please!"

An expression falling somewhere between being impressed and insulted crosses Decaux's face. I'm sure Claudia's demanding tone doesn't sit well with him. My wolf issues a snarl beyond even what I can control. Just the thought of Decaux touching Claudia sends my sense of protection in flux.

"Ugh! Just give it to her, dad," Dacari sighs, taking the stone from her father and placing it in Claudia's hand. Once more winking at Brian, Dacari whispers, "I got you, babe," and goes back to Decaux's side.

As soon as Claudia takes the stones in her hands, a luminous blue light shines through the den and her eyes shimmer with a bright blue hue.

"Claudia!" I shout as I watch her go still as the power of the stones takes hold of her. Pulling myself from Brian's grip, I take Claudia's shoulders in my hands, shaking her.

She remains enchanted, her eyes frozen blue.

I reach for the stones, hoping to pry them out of her hands, but Jackson pulls my hand back.

"No, Mark!" Jackson shouts. "It's too late. By her own word, she is either bound to truth or death."

"That's right young one," Decaux calmly says, coming to my side. "You only get three questions, so be specific. Ask only what you need to know."

Swallowing hard, thoughts of anything happening to Claudia pain through the entirety of me. Despite everything, just as I knew that night the tree trunk almost crushed her while she slept, I know without a doubt I couldn't bear to see any harm come to her. Even if it's revealed that she tried to hurt Jerrica, and as painful as it is to admit it to myself, I know I will always love Claudia.

The truth is, I never stopped loving her. At this point, I can say I never will.

Taking a deep breath, I blink hard, hopeful to push my impending tears aside. It's time to get the truth once and for all.

Chapter 33

"Oh all of this posturing and ancient stone nonsense is ridiculous! Will someone just go through her things and get my blade!" Chartreuse shouts.

"Now, now," Decaux quickly counters, as his vampiric speed carries him in front of Chartreuse. "Before you even think to siren your charms against us, it would do you well to recall your charms won't work on me, dear. My brother sired you and you're of my bloodline. So is Dacari. And if what she's done to mere Scourge vampires is any indication of her power, I think it unwise to put her powers to the test against you, my dear Chartreuse." If the slithering, threatening tone of Decaux's words alone weren't enough to douse any untoward motives of Chartreuse, the way he's leaning into her, as his long fingers grip her neck sends a clear message. He will end her if need be. And I'm sure he'd do so without a lick of remorse.

While a part of me is somewhat thankful for his actions, I'm no fool. We'll certainly be indebted to Decaux once this is all said and done.

"Mark." Jackson's calm tone turns me to him. "Are you sure you can do this? I can help if need be." Although I'm appreciative for Jackson's offer. I need to do this myself.

Wiggling in Decaux's grip, Chartreuse hisses, "Just get me my blade! Then I'll be out of your way."

"Oh you'll stay right here, dear one. Until I say so," Decaux digs a long nail against the ravine of Chartreuse's neck. Looking back over his shoulder, he nods to Jackson.

"I can do it," I answer Jackson.

Taking a deep breath as I take Claudia's shoulders in my hands, I look into her frozen glare. Seeing her like this pains me more than it probably should. But it's time to get the truth out.

"Remember Mark, you only get a few questions," Dacari says from behind me. "Once the light flickers you'll know the time is up."

"But if the stone fades to black—" Brian begins.

"She dies." I interrupt him. My eyes turn to mist just at the thought of anything happening to her.

Placing his palm on my shoulder, Jackson's calm manner is exactly what I need. "Take your time, Lord Helsing. We're here with you." With a comforting smile, his soothing tone eases my angst.

Heaving a sigh, I turn my attention back to Claudia.

"Claudia, can you hear me?" I start, searching her face. Still, her expression remains entranced by the stone. Her eyes, covered in a luminous blue, give me no assurance she even understands what's happening.

Thankfully, she grants me a small nod, letting me know it's safe to proceed.

"On the night when Jerrica Jeffers—"

"Oh for mercy, Decaux! Must I yet again endure a lament for the cause of poor, sweet, Jerrica?" Chartreuse whines with a shrilling lilt.

Decaux tightens his hold around her neck and leans into her with his forearm. "I swear to you Chartreuse, I will not hesitate to end you right now!" he bites back.

"Dad please!" Dacari yells back, stepping forward. I don't turn to see her, but I can tell she's now at Brian's side. "Let Lord Helsing finish."

"Yes, Marchand," Jackson adds. "Once the process has started—"

"Only if this little crooning minx promises to keep quiet!" He warns as his eyes flash with their crimson glow. "I already saved you once when you were the cause of Jerrica's peril, dear one. I shall not render such a mercy to you again!"

A series of hissing and snarls play out between the two until Chartreuse finally concedes to Decaux's will. Writhing desperately beneath his fierce grip I see the malice behind her eyes, and it becomes clearer to me than ever. Chartreuse truly loathes Jerrica.

Pushing the thought aside, I look into my mate's icy blue eyes. A hard lump swells in my throat making my next words painful to utter. "Claudia, on the night in question did you attempt to kill Jerrica Jeffers?"

Chartreuse sighs dismissively. "Oh out with it already, girl!"

"No." Claudia answers and there is no lilt in her tone.

My eyes widen with hope at her reveal, and I look over my shoulder at Jackson. He offers only a restrained grin, but nods for me to continue.

"No, I did not try to kill Jerrica," she affirms, still staring straightway.

"Lies!" Both Brian and Chartreuse cry out in unison.

A sheepish frown covers Brian's face when he realizes he and Chartreuse agree. Chartreuse, however, releases a shrieking cackle in response. Decaux's hold on her lessens as he, too, looks at me in disbelief.

"What more do you want?" I bark at Brian. I could care less what Chartreuse thinks. "She has the stone in her hand! She answered the question!"

"Perhaps you're asking the wrong question, dear," Chartreuse snickers devilishly as Decaux once more pins her against the wall. This time, she seems more amused than before.

"She's right," Brian agrees with his hands lifted in caution. Even he has to know how ridiculous he sounds agreeing with the likes of Chartreuse Grenoble. "I mean just because she didn't stab Jerrica doesn't mean she wasn't in cahoots with Colin and Chartreuse."

"The only person who should be on trial here is that murderous leech!" I holler, pointing at Chartreuse. I refuse to continue to entertain the notion of Claudia's guilt. "Why must you persist with this witch hunt?"

"Ask again!" Jackson commands. More than annoyed with it all, I can see his patience has all but waned.

Acknowledging with a slight bow, I turn back to Claudia. But not before flashing my eyes in warning to Brian. I need him to back the fuck off. Reining in my frustration, a low growl permeates through me, and I let out a heavy sigh.

Taking her face in my palms, I allow my thumb to strum her jawline. Just the touch of her skin eases the tension I feel of my wolf bucking beneath my flesh.

"Claudia, baby, please tell me, who stabbed Jerrica?"

Groaning, the light flickers as Claudia's mouth quivers. She shakes and her eyes dim then brighten once more. This must be more painful for her than I can imagine. Crap!

"This is hurting her!" I yell to Jackson over my shoulder.

"Because she knows the truth, my lord." Brian mumbles.

"You have to keep going, young one." The cajoling tenor of Decaux's tone is surprising. Casting an almost sympathetic gaze, his eyes soften as he regards me.

Quivering once more, Claudia quakes in my grasp and the light flashes bright.

Turning back to her, I try again. "Baby, it doesn't matter what you tell me. I know now it won't change how I feel about you. Do you hear me? Nothing you say changes anything between us, baby. Everything that happened this week was real to me. Everything I said. Everything. You are more than my mate, Claudia. You are my life. You always have been, Lady Helsing."

"Mark, no!" Brian pleads, coming to my side. He works hard to catch my attention, but I keep my eyes locked on Claudia.

"Stand back, Brian!" Jackson roars. "That's an order!"

Brian steps back, taking heavy breaths as he does.

The room remains quiet as everyone awaits Claudia's reply.

Slowly, her shivering subsides and the flickering light of the stone settles back to its blue hue. Her eyes remain icy blue, but when I see one lone tear fall to her chin, I know whatever she has to say next is harder than even I can imagine.

"It's all right, Claudia. I'm here, baby," I say, using my thumb to wipe away her tears.

"Oh how sweet," Chartreuse sneers from beneath Decaux's tight hold. "It's touching how much you love her. Truly it is. But the fact remains, my blade allows no folly. Whether this wretched stone is truly a broker of truth as you all believe remains to be seen." Laughing, her high-pitched cackling sound pierces the ears of every wolf in the room.

"What do you mean?" Jackson questions, stepping just shy of Chartreuse and Decaux.

A grim expression covers Decaux's face as he looks over his shoulder to Jackson. "Sure the stone may be a seeker of truth. But Chartreuse's blade provides more forensic analysis than any tool of men."

"Meaning?" I sigh, wanting to just get this over.

"Meaning, my dear, my blade knows whether blood was shed. And I can tell you this, blood has in fact been spilled by your beloved. Despite whatever this ancient stone suggests."

Chartreuse's words grip my soul just as tight as Decaux's hand is wrenched around her neck. Every time I think I can take a breath from this nonsense, some new piece of information tightens its grip on the whole of me.

Sucking in a breath, I do my best to shake off Chartreuse's claims.

"My father," Claudia whispers. Another stream of tears floods her face.

"Your father? Did Colin stab Jerrica?"

Shaking once more, her lips quiver. "Yes. My father stabbed Jerrica." Continuing to quake in my hold, the light in her hand flickers.

"You don't have much time, Lord Helsing!" Dacari cries out.

"That's it! You all heard her! Colin stabbed Jerrica!" I yell.

Coming into my view, Brian snarls, but I can tell he's working hard to steady himself. "But you heard Chartreuse! Claudia does have blood on her hands. You have to finish this!"

"Finish it, young one!" Decaux exclaims while Chartreuse stares on.

Jackson only nods in affirmation, and as much as it hurts

me to even think of pushing her too far, a part of me knows Claudia is innocent. Despite all claims to the contrary, I know I can trust my wolf. I know what I shared with Claudia these last few days wasn't a fluke. What we shared was real.

Not only do I know I can trust my wolf. I now know with all certainty, I can trust my heart.

Chapter 34

Kissing the crown of her head, I press my forehead to hers. "It's okay, beautiful. Just tell me what happened."

The light brightens some, its blue luminesce remains as Claudia's shaking ceases. "My father stabbed Jerrica. And I stabbed my father."

Stepping back, my eyes widen in shock. Claudia's reveal surprises me. Now, I am speechless.

Releasing another shrilling cackle, Chartreuse is the only one amused. Even Decaux seems confounded.

Searching Claudia's face, I wish I could see her bright green eyes looking back at me. I tire of this blue haze. I know what Claudia looks like when she lies. I don't need a stone to tell me anything. But the stone doesn't fade to black, so I know she is truthful.

"But why, Claudia?" I breathe back, still stumped.

"It's all I could do to stop him. He was a man possessed. Chartreuse charmed him. I didn't know anything about his plans to kill Jerrica. When I saw him stab her, I pulled his arm, hopeful to stop him. But he was strong. His eyes dazzled with a glow I've only ever known when Chartreuse muses someone. I pleaded with him to stop, but he wouldn't. He kept daggering her. We tussled. Somehow as I was pulling the knife from my father, I stabbed him. I stabbed him! I killed my father! That's what I was trying to tell you, Mark! I'm so sorry. I killed my father! I deserve to die!" Crumpling at her waist, Claudia wails hard as the memory of that night tears her in two.

Dropping the stones to floor, her desperate cries continue. I swoop her into my arms just before she falls to the ground. Cradling her, I hold Claudia close to my chest. Stinging tears sear my skin when I can no longer hold back my own sobbing streams.

"I've got you, baby," I whisper, kissing her cheek and holding her tight. Looking around the room, a rumbling growl pains through me. "What more do you want from her?" I shout to our onlookers.

The solemn expression now covering Brian's face is the first I see. He now knows he has been wrong about Claudia the entire time. Stepping back, Brian plummets into the sofa, his shoulders slumped in shame. Dacari, pats his back, consoling him. It's a good thing he has her to do so, because he'll not get an ounce of consolation from me.

"Calm yourself, young alpha," Jackson says, now blocking my view of Brian. "The truth is out now. Your mate is safe."

"My lord she is more than my mate. Lady Helsing will be more than a mate to breed, she will be my wife."

An appreciative grin covers Jackson's face, and his eyes almost seem to dance. I know of anyone in this room, my Prime Alpha is indeed happy for me. Even though I know he may feel some remorse, I know Brian doesn't share Jackson's sentiment.

"Well, there is no need to entertain these issues further. So I suggest—"

"I suggest you find my blade!" Chartreuse lashes, breaking from Decaux's hold. "Should I have to go without my blade another day, those creatures for which you currently contend will seem like daffodils compared to the havoc I'll shed upon the entirety of New Orleans!"

"She's right!" Decaux adds, using his arm to hold her back. "Her dagger is enchanted to keep her feeding at minimal. Should she continue without it—"

Groaning, Claudia works to sit up in my lap. "I told you Chartreuse I don't have it. Stone or no stone, that's the truth."

"Then you lie, girl!" Chartreuse sneers. "I know the call of my own blade as I would that of my own blood. Just as I knew you shed blood by the hand of my blade. If only I knew you sought the life of your own father! You stupid girl! I would kill to have my father—I'd give anything—"

"Well, you can follow him to the pit for all I care!" Claudia growls and her eyes flash bright gold.

"Baby, don't let her get to you. She'll follow him in due time I'm sure," I say, hopeful to turn Claudia's attention away from Chartreuse.

Claudia's posture softens slightly in my hold, but she keeps her sights on Chartreuse. "You know while it was never my intention to kill my father, I'll tell you this; I do not mourn him. Sure the thought of taking a life pains me more than a murderous soul like you can fathom, but I do not share the same regard for my father that you do of yours. Because what kind of father tries to sell his daughter to the highest bidder!" Claudia shouts.

"What the—" I gasp, but barely get the words out when Claudia starts making her way off the floor. Holding her forearms, I pull her up and steady her arm around my waist.

Slowly circling the sofa, Dacari steps out from behind Brian. "Claudia, what are you saying?"

"I'm saying that once Dalcour turned down my father's dowry offer—which included me—he made his rounds through the faction. He offered me like I was mere property to any Altrinion-vampire he thought would have me. His desire to steep his lineage in Altrinion blood grew incessant over the years. When Dalcour turned me down, he turned to that wretched Caius Agrippa and Lord Titan! I pleaded with him not to but—"

"Lord Titan?" Chartreuse quietly asks, this time her expression is softer than normal. Placing her small hands on Decaux's arm, she looks at him, hopeful he'll let her free. Almost reticent, he does, but keeps at her side.

"Yes, but you'll be happy to know he turned my father down," Claudia says in a low tone. Chartreuse smiles and for the first time, a genuine gleam of happiness meets her eyes.

"That makes me happy indeed." Chartreuse's calm tone is almost surprising. But we've all heard the rumors of her affections for Titan over the years. Although he normally comes across as just another philandering scoundrel, one would almost think there's a reason this news pleases Chartreuse. "Well, dearest, I suppose you are the first woman to do what I only wish I had the strength to do centuries ago. Whether you choose to admit it to yourself or not, my girl, there was something inside you refusing to succumb to the will of men. And while the path I chose may seem wrought with villainous intent, never doubt my reasons were to ensure you, dear one, would never endure my fate." The gentleness of Chartreuse's tone is strangely unnerving. Such a sentiment from someone as heinous as Chartreuse is hard to digest.

Nothing but a sheer look of surprise spreads across the faces of each of us assembled in the den. For the first time since everyone arrived, the space doesn't feel as suffocating as before. Another dewy mist covers the room and I slowly see the sheen of luster cover the area, brightening the entirety of the den.

Taking Claudia's hand in hers, Chartreuse offers a smile that once more reaches her eyes. "Claudia, listen, now that you have secured your fate it's time you secure your heart. Goodness knows I never thought I'd see the day when my bloodline would mingle with that of wolf blood, but you have indeed made a believer out of me. And for as long as you share your life with this alpha of the Dunes Pack of Beta Primes, I swear no harm shall come to them by my hand or any of my brood. That, my girl, I swear to you."

Claudia looks over her shoulder at me, cracking a stunned smile. "Thank you, Chartreuse."

"Now if I could just retrieve my blade I can be on my way," Chartreuse says, stepping back. Her face darkens, and I can tell whatever barter she made is tenuous at best.

"I already told you. I don't have it," Claudia says under her breath.

"And she doesn't need it!" Brian barks back, jumping up from his seat.

"Easy, Brian!" Dacari warns as she sees Chartreuse's eyes blacken.

"Claudia may be innocent, but the fact remains that Chartreuse is not! She not only mused Colin, but devised a plan to kill Jerrica. She needs to pay for her crimes. The last thing she needs is a dagger to finish the job she had Colin start!" Brian lashes, lunging at Chartreuse.

Shaking his head in warning, Decaux jumps in between

Brian and Chartreuse. This time Decaux backs his arm to Brian, not Chartreuse, in warning.

"Oh you have nothing to fear from me, dearest!" Chartreuse snaps. "Every pain I wish to inflict on Jerrica has already taken root. Death would be too easy for her. While I was not there to witness her downfall—oh and I wish I were—think it not strange that she never absolved Claudia. Jerrica alone knew Claudia had nothing to do with the attempt on her life, but she let it stand. And she did so as a means of retaliation on me and my bloodline. All because her frail ego can't stand to know the love of her life chose me over her. But that is another story for another time. Now move out of my way before you cause me to renege vows I just made to Lady Helsing and her young alpha."

Brian grumbles hard and I see the fur along his forearm thicken.

"Stand down, Brian! That is an order!" I shout, stepping to Chartreuse's side.

"Will you now align yourself with her after all her aggressions?"

Growling, I place myself square before Brian. "She has shown no aggression here!"

Brian's eyes flash gold, but the deep growl of my wolf forces him to submission and he takes a step back. Snarling, he fights his own willpower hard.

Coming to Brian's side, Dacari wraps her small hands around his bicep. "It's okay, Brian. Today's battle has already been won." Taking his chin, she turns him so that only she is in his view. Uttering a phrase in the ancient tongue, Dacari's words seem to quiet his storm.

Brian closes his eyes and takes a deep breath.

Looking over her shoulder, Chartreuse winks at Decaux. "Impressive Marchand! These women surely know how to bend the will of men. And your little one is rather remarkable indeed! But I suppose you'll see me again since you refuse to produce my blade. Which is unfortunate since—"

"I—I have it," Lorien calls from the doorway. With the blade in his palms, he stands fearful of Chartreuse's next move.

"Lorien, how did you get her dagger?" I ask, making my way to the door.

Shrugging his shoulders, his nervous eyes bounce around the room, but I step square in front of him, keeping his gaze fixed on me.

"Well, when we found Claudia she had the knife on her. We took it from her. But I didn't think it was safe to leave it at the mansion or the Tavern. I thought it was better if I kept it with us. I'm sorry if I messed up."

Squeezing his shoulder, I offer him the same reassuring smile Jackson always gives me. "No, Lorien, you did nothing wrong." Taking the dagger from him, I turn to Chartreuse. "I know doing this is teetering between doing the wrong thing and the worst thing, but I can think of no better resolve. I only hope you keep your word to leave my wolves free of whatever sinister dealings you may have."

Placing the dagger in her palm, her blackened eyes return to their greenish hue. "Oh I assure you, young alpha as long as the smile I see on my kin remains, you shall have no fear of me." Quickly placing the blade in her holster, Chartreuse offers me a brief nod.

Issuing a low, musing hum, she uses her vampiric speed and makes her way toward Claudia. Everyone in the room except Decaux, Dacari, Claudia, and myself are frozen, entranced by the tune of her voice. For a moment I fear she bested me and I need to attack, but when I look at Decaux, he lifts his palm in caution, warning me not to act on my impulse.

"Dear one," Chartreuse begins, taking Claudia's face in her hands. "You are truly what I hoped to be. I am not, nor shall I ever be of such a pure heart. When I saved my sister Chalmette all those years ago it was for this moment. I only wished she could live to see it. And while you are only a remnant of what she left behind, for the first time, I feel hopeful that all my toils were not in vain. Take care of yourself, young one. Stay close to your mate and never let him go. A love as pure as what you two share will be tested. But do what you must to see it endure."

And with a quick peck on Claudia's cheek, Chartreuse exits the den, freeing everyone from their catatonic state at her departure.

Chapter 35

Claudia wastes no time using what's left of her energy to sprint across the room, leaping into my embrace. Tossing her arms around my neck, Claudia kisses my cheek. "I love you, Mark!" she cries into my chest. "I love you so much!"

Kissing the top of her head, I hold her tight. "It's okay, baby. I love you too! I got you now!"

Leaning back, I'm surprised to find Claudia's glassy eyes are full of worry. "I'm so sorry I didn't just tell you everything. But I had to make her think I was on her side. I couldn't risk her musing me like she did my father or—"

Placing my forefinger on her sweet lips, I kiss her forehead and smile. "It's okay baby," I laugh. "I don't think she can charm women. From what I'm told, sirens can't hurt women. You were always safe, beautiful."

Claudia's brows furrow, but she lets me pull her back into my hold.

I look over Claudia's shoulder at Decaux, and the grim expression on his face tells me I may be wrong. He shakes his head, darting his eyes to Dacari. Although she and Brian are in an intense huddle of sorts, I can tell he doesn't want Dacari knowing whatever Claudia may reveal. Acknowledging with a slight nod, I turn my attention back to Claudia.

"Listen baby, I don't want to think about Chartreuse for another minute! She's taken enough from us for one day, don't you think?" Pulling her face to mine, I crush my mouth to hers.

Feeling Claudia relax in my arms is everything. I could hold her like this forever. Too bad we have company.

"Why don't we give the happy couple a little time alone?" Jackson's voice breaks through the intensity of our kiss.

Claudia relaxes at my side as I wrap my arms around her shoulder, holding her tight.

"Yes, yes," Decaux begins, making his way toward us. "I am certainly no fan of long farewells. But one day very soon I shall collect on all of the benevolence bestowed upon you today, young alpha," he coolly remarks on his way out. Stopping at the threshold, he turns back to me and Claudia. Narrowing his eyes with a cagey grin to match, he rubs the stubble on his jaw and laughs. "While everyone likes to give my brother Dalcour credit for assisting the Dunes wolves it has always been my desire to see the rightful restoration of your kind. Just as I was a friend to your father, Abraham, and his father before him, I shall endeavor to share the same kindness to you for as long as I am able." Primping the brim of his hat, he offers a quick wink and looks into the den. "Dacari, dear, we mustn't dally. We still need to clean up our mess. I'm sure we can afford these mates one more night of bliss before we require his aid."

Turning on his heel, Decaux's long black trench coat flairs wide as he makes his exit. He certainly has quite a flair for the dramatic, just as Dalcour has always said.

Walking hand in hand, Dacari and Brian make their way to

the door. Dacari hugs Claudia as Brian stands quietly behind her. His eyes wander to mine for a second but he quickly lowers them, likely afraid to look me in the eye.

"Listen hun, I know we don't know each other, but I suppose we should get to know one another soon. I'm pretty sure there'll be some double dating in our future," Dacari laughs, placing a small kiss on Claudia's cheek.

Claudia smiles wide and I see her eyes twinkle. "Yes, let's make that happen!" It's been so long since she's had a close female relationship, the thought of her and Dacari hanging out sounds cool.

"I'll call you!" Dacari smiles, waving at both of us as she leaves.

Brian remains inside with his head low. "I need to apologize. I am sorry for how I acted. My actions are indeed regrettable."

Claudia pokes out her bottom lip, lifting her big bright eyes at me, tugging my heart strings.

"Listen, B, it's okay. This has been a crazy time for all of us. No apologies needed. Let's just all move on from here."

"Thank you, my lord," Brian mutters. "But I wasn't speaking to you," he adds looking up at Claudia.

Both mine and Claudia's eyes widen in shock but our mouths part in surprise when Brian drops to his knees before us.

"Brian, what are you doing?" Claudia gasps, stepping back.

Brian is a big man. Almost as wide as two doors, with a brawn, deity-like body to match. For as big as he is, even on the floor his size alone is intimidating. Especially in the presence of Claudia's small five-foot four frame.

"I'm sorry, my lady. I know I offended you. Not only did I not trust my alpha, but I also didn't trust you. I'd be a complete hypocrite if I said I trusted my alpha, but refused to trust who he trusts."

Taking his shoulder in her small palm, she squeezes it just enough for him to look up at her. "Look Brian, I know I haven't been the easiest over the years. But all of that is behind us now. Besides, if nothing else at least I know I can trust you with our alpha. If you'll challenge me, I know you'd gladly take on any challenger. It's that type of loyalty that will help me sleep at night. I need to know Mark is surrounded by people he can trust. I know he can trust you."

"With my whole life," Brian roars back, pounding his chest with his fist.

Planting another kiss on Claudia's forehead, I can't help smiling. Seeing her and Brian at peace, makes my heart happy. These are two of my favorite people in the world. And goodness knows my world wouldn't be right if these two remained at odds.

"So I turn my back for a minute and you're already on your knees making promises to another woman?" Dacari teases from the doorpost. She gives Claudia a quick wink as she twists her braids into a bun. Claudia covers her mouth, trying to shield her laughter.

"Um, Cari I was just—I needed to apologize—"

"Oh that's okay, babe. I'm just taking note. You like to apologize to women on your knees. Good to know," she taunts him, biting her bottom lip. The two share a look, and Claudia and I look away and try not to laugh. It's going to take some getting used to seeing the Big Bad Wolf himself tongue-tied over a woman. Especially, Dacari Peyroux. This will be interesting to see how it plays out.

"Yeah, I think that's your cue, B," I say, offering my hand to him.

Wiping the dust from his pant leg, he grumbles, likely annoyed at his dirt stain. "Again, my apologies, my lord. And please know I understand if you need to charge someone else as your second. I've challenged you far too many times. I wouldn't blame you if—"

"Nonsense!" I protest, turning my head with my palms raised. "As Claudia said, you're the only one I trust to do so. Now all we need to do is just trust each other."

"Yes, my lord," Brian says, taking my shoulder in his hand.

Pulling Brian's forearm, I throw my arms around his hulking frame. "Aww shucks, bring it in brother!"

Clapping his hands hard, Jackson comes to our side, patting me and Brian on our backs. "This is exactly the type of brotherhood I want to see in our dens. We can't be afraid to disagree from time to time, only as long as this is the end result!"

The three of us share a hearty laugh and I can even feel my wolf warm inside. Even he's happy. Looking over both Jackson and Brian's large frames, I'm happy to see Dacari and Claudia whispering with one another along the threshold.

"Now, let's allow these two some privacy. I mean we did interrupt them after all. And technically, Lord Helsing has until tomorrow's moon rising to make everything official. I'll send Dranoel to get you tomorrow as planned. In the meantime, the rest of us will join Decaux and Dacari in cleaning the streets of this new vermin and any Scourge we detect. You two, however, should resume—your um—duties."

Chapter 36

nd return to our duties we have.

Looking at her perfect body laying beneath me now, I am overcome with a joy I never thought I'd find again. Holding her legs in the air by her ankles, everything I've ever wanted is in my view.

With my free hand, I tease her entrance with my tip and the sound of her sweet arousal makes my heart race. But it's the pure gleam of desire in Claudia's eyes assuring me she wants nothing more than to feel me dive into her depths.

Jutting her hips up, she pulls me in, forcing me to dip my leading inside her sweet hole. "Mark, please!" she pleads, gyrating until she has the fullness of my manhood within her.

"Damn, baby!" I cry out as the sheer ecstasy of how good she feels makes the hair on my forearms stand. I never knew anything could feel so good, but now that I know, I'll never let her go.

Driving myself deep in long, hard strokes, the loud growls roaring between us as she meets my thrusts tell me my baby wants this as much as I do.

"Hit it, Mark! Right there, baby! Ahh… hit it!" Claudia moans as her hands scale the small of my back. Her eyes flash wide when I mercilessly pound her pearl, grinding into her as hard as I can.

"I'm gonna make it hurt, baby. You're gonna feel me in you for a week!" I roar, slamming into her sweet place.

"Ahh! Mark! Please!" she cries out, writhing beneath me, still gripping my back. "I feel it baby! I feel it!"

"On your knees!" I order, slipping out of her.

She does as I instruct, but when I see her lift her ass in the air my instinct drives me wild. Smacking her backside, and watching it jiggle just for me, I grab my shaft, rubbing it hard. Looking at her sweet hole, glistening and wet, I run my finger along her folds, drawing out her nectar. Sucking my finger, just the scent of her arousal forces beads of cum from my crown.

"I just love looking at you like this, beautiful!" I groan, circling my finger around her entrance.

Arching her back, she bounces up and down, allowing me to see inside her depths as she does. Looking over her shoulder, she bites her lips, pleased to see me getting off on just the bounce of her ass and my view of her sweet spot.

"Like what you see?" she breathes, licking her lips. Pushing her hips back, she hikes her bottom higher, then lowers it, before shaking it once more.

"You like teasing me?" I grunt, grabbing her hips. Plunging my hard girth back inside her, she gasps, buckling at her knees, but I keep my hold on her hips. "You like showing me what's mine?"

"Yes, baby, yes," Claudia whines, as I tug her hair while driving myself in and out of her.

"Good, because you're gonna show it to me every day! Do you understand?"

"Yes," she cries out as I rotate my hips, grinding deep.

"This is my home! I'm gonna live in this sweet little hole! Every time I see it, I'm gonna fuck it because I can! And you're gonna let me in here! Aren't you?"

"It's your home, make yourself comfortable, baby!"

Slamming in and out of her, all I think about is that she mine. This sweet pearl is mine. *Her heart is mine.* But I am also hers. And as much as I want to be a selfish lover, I can't be selfish with her.

Slowly sliding out of her, I flip her over on top of me and bring her mouth to mine. Tethering our tongues tight, our kiss is as passionate as ever. The sweetness of Claudia's tongue knows no bounds as she explores my mouth, owning every inch. Her tiny fingers lock into my beard and I'm sure my baby likes controlling this moment more than I can understand.

Sliding down on my shaft, Claudia cries out as she slowly grinds on me. She brings my hands to her breasts, keeping them in place as she bounces up and down. Claudia knows how much I enjoy seeing her plump rack mesmerize me as she moves.

Bucking me hard, I feel her pulsing center lock its hold on my girth. Her eyes widen and her sexy mouth drips open as she sits on the edge of her orgasm. "Oh! Oh! Mark!"

"That's right, baby! Let it go! Let your fountain pour over me," I say, pushing myself up and deeper into her sweet center.

Screaming my name, her arousal drips along my length and onto my thighs. Convulsing as she does, I plunge into her hard, releasing my own stream of ecstasy within her. Pulling her close, so that her body is pressed against mine, the feel of our sweet stickiness meshed between us makes me smile.

Holding Claudia as she rests on my chest feels so damn good. Kissing her forehead, she wiggles a bit, but her eyes widen with surprise as she looks up at me. "Baby," she moans, and her eyes fall to the side. "You're still hard," she says in shock while rocking along my tip.

A smug smirk covers my face as I feel myself harden even more as she works herself against me. "You've got an alpha, sweetheart. Not some mortal man who shrivels up after a release. Now slide that pretty little pearl back down on me. I love seeing how beautiful you look when I'm filling your sweet hole."

Claudia casts a sexy little smirk all her own before gliding her fine body down on me. "Then fill me up, baby," she moans. Wincing a bit as she reaches my base, she slowly grinds into me.

"Does it hurt?" I ask, worried. I don't want to cause her any pain.

Leaning into my chest, she keeps grinding and the motion nearly drives me wild. Grabbing her backside, I reach around and find the connection of us there. I touch her slick folds and she lets out a pleasurable moan as I do. But when I expand my hands along my girth, I realize just how much I'm stretching her.

She groans as I touch her there and I feel more wetness drip along my fingertips.

"It hurts so good, baby. Please keep fucking me, Mark. I need it! This is what I've always needed!" She cries out.

Lifting her chin, I look at her and am surprised to see actual tears.

"Baby what's wrong?" I say, holding her steady.

Once more taking my hand in hers, she moves my hand along her body, landing on her perfect breasts. Pressing my thumb to her nipples as I know she likes, she moans, circling her hips so that I hit her spot.

"Claudia?" I call her name. I need to know what my baby needs.

"For years all I wanted was this. *Us*," she admits, still gyrating on me. "The happiest I've ever been is with you Mark. That's why when we were apart, I thought I needed to harden my heart. But this—this feels so good. So free. I feel like I can finally be me again. The way you look at me. The way you make me feel—this is all I ever wanted."

Sitting up, I lean my back against the wall, straddling Claudia around my waist. "Oh baby, don't cry. I promise I'm not going anywhere corazón."

Taking my face in her palms, Claudia continues milling her softness against my rock-hard shaft. "I'm so sorry, Mark. I know now I should've trusted you completely. I put more faith in a stone than in our love. For so long every move I made was done in fear. I should have known I could trust you with all of me. So from here on out, that's what you're going to get, baby. You're getting all of me!"

Calling out my name, Claudia's tidal wave of passion erupts all over me once more. Locking her in my embrace, she leans into my hold. Crying as she nestles herself at the nape of my neck, her pulsing center grips me perfectly as I run my fingers through her hair.

"That's it baby, let it all out. I've got you," I whisper into her ear. "Just let me take care of you from now on. I will do all I can to make myself worthy of your trust. Sit right here on my lap and let me take care of you and this pretty little pearl and your beautiful heart," I add, taking hold of one of her breasts. Flicking my thumb against her nipple, she moans while cradling deeper into my embrace.

Sitting back, I lean my head against the wall and let out small chuckle. Shaking my head, the thought racing through my mind right now, makes me laugh.

Looking up at me with her big, bright eyes, Claudia sits up. We both grunt at the pleasurable feel of her motion, knowing we'll likely be locked like this for the remainder of the day. "What's so funny?" she asks.

"Well, the thought crossed my mind once before, but now—now I think I understand it all," I laugh.

"What, Mark? Tell me."

"For the last four years while we were a part, I wondered why you seemed mad all the time. Now it all makes sense." She frowns, puzzled, but I trail my hand through her hair, smiling. "I'm just happy we're together now. I don't think the world can take you walking around angrily horny all the time. It's a good thing you've got me now."

Laughing, she kisses my cheek and smiles. "That's right, Lord Helsing. I've got you now and I'm never letting you go. Besides, it's my job to keep the light on for you," she says adding a small kiss.

"Oh, beautiful, I thought you knew. You are my light."

Chapter 37

"*We rise and fall... together,*" Claudia and I say in unison.

Standing before more than fifty prime and pack wolves from all over, we clasp our hands together as we look out into the crowd. Bright wolfen eyes stare back at us, gleaming with smiles and lifting harmonious howls as we stand before them.

"I present to you, Lord and Lady Helsing," Jackson announces to a cheerful chorus. "And with their proclamation of marriage, the two are forever bound in both love and covenant. The two are now one. As you see him, you see her. As you honor him, you do so honor her. As he is your alpha, so does she bear with him in all things. With exception to his wolfen form, they are alike in all ways of man."

Another series of howls and roars echo throughout the wooded lot and it's music to my ears. The harmonic cadence of each wolf chimes in my ear and I can make out every distinction. Pounding their chest, they kneel in submission and Jackson turns to me, gesturing for me to step forward.

Claudia moves with me but releases my hand almost instinctively as I make my way to the center of the crowd. Briefly looking over my shoulder to her and Jackson, I smile as I look up when I see the moon come out from behind the clouds.

Yelping aloud, I feel my muscles contort beneath my skin and my breathing quickens. Thick fur forms along my forearm, and my canines lengthen. Growling, my chest heaves up and down. One more growl and my wolf breaks through the barrier of my skin, forcing me to the ground on all fours.

Howling, the remainder of wolves echo my call as they begin to shift.

Turning about, I find Claudia standing with Jackson and Dacari. Claudia's eyes flash to gold as she stares at me. Issuing another yelp in her direction, she looks at me and smiles. Mouthing *"I love you,"* in reply, my heart warms knowing she even understands me in wolfen form.

Roaring aloud, the packs howl in reply and I leap atop a large boulder. Five alphas and five den leaders gather five wolves to their side as we prepare to head out on the hunt. Brian and Dilano remain with me as I commission the packs to round up and destroy both the Scourge and rabid creatures. Each group will travel through the entirety of Louisiana and the borders of Mississippi to ensure we contain the threat they pose.

Our Prime Alpha bellows one final growl while Claudia and Dacari echo a ceremonious howl all their own. Once more, my heart nearly thumps out of my chest just hearing the cadence of my beloved's call. Not only has she seamlessly stepped into her role as my mate, but she was also undoubtedly made for this.

And while going out to face the creatures who threaten our world is hardly what I thought our first days as husband and wife should be, knowing Claudia is in my life gives me all the strength I need to ensure I come back home to her.

Because truly, there is no other place I'd rather be.

Epilogue

"Okay you have our attention," Decaux grumbles as he saunters casually in front of the window. Admiring the sliver of sunlight beaming along his shoulder, something tells me he's still in awe of his ability to walk in the sun once again. "What was so urgent you needed to beckon us to your throne room?" He adds, dismissively waving his arm around the parlor.

"Please, Decaux," Jackson frowns, giving Decaux a hard stare. "Lord Helsing obviously has something of importance to share. We owe him our attention." Turning back to me, Jackson leans against the doorpost, and gestures his hand for me to speak.

Although he's my Prime Alpha, even his gesturing feels a bit odd. Over the last two weeks, I've made myself quite at home as alpha. So much so that I've taken over residency at the Marchand mansion. As odd as it sometimes feels to walk along the M insignia along marble stoned hallway it was always Dalcour's intent to give the mansion to me once I proved my rank. In fact, he even had Jerrica and Braelyn draw up the covenants to ensure as much was recorded with the city. Not only have I not needed permission to do as I please in the mansion and in the city for that matter, but I recognize Decaux's jab regarding my throne room for what it is.

It's his snide way of reminding me I am indebted to the Marchands.

If I didn't have another reason to get this over with, I know having Jackson, Decaux, and Brian in a room together too long is like tempting fate. There are way too many egos in this room for me to linger a minute longer. If it weren't for Claudia and Dacari's presence, I can't fathom how tense the room would feel. Thankfully, everyone is playing nice in front of the ladies.

Standing up from my seat, Claudia rises with me as we walk hand in hand to the center of the parlor.

"Thank you all for coming. I'll do my best to keep this brief," I begin.

"Splendid!" Decaux sneers, twirling his fingers along the shade cord on the window.

Jarring her elbow into her father's side, Dacari's eye's flash like a bright white light. "Dad, please!"

Laughing and throwing his arm around her shoulder, Decaux sighs a bit while trying to restrain himself. "My apologies, Lord Helsing, please continue."

Brian issues a low snarl but keeps his attention on me. It's clear he's trying to remain neutral. I doubt he wants to ruffle matters between his beloved and her father.

Squeezing my hand, Claudia gives me a reassuring nod, and it's just the push I need. "As I was saying, I've asked you here because I believe more dangers exist beyond the threat of the undead, rabid creatures roaming our streets."

"You have our attention," Brian adds, folding his arms across his chest.

"Thank you, B," I smile. I'm glad to have Brian and me on the same side once again. "But actually, I think I should let

Claudia explain."

Claudia gives me a small smile and I nod for her to speak. "Thank you, my lord," she starts, as she casts her gaze around the room and back to me. "As you all know when Chartreuse came for her blade, I maintained my pretense that I was on her side until I was able to have the stones. I did so because I feared that she could charm me to do her bidding just as she had done to my father. I feared should she not see me as an ally, she'd seek no other recourse than to set her muse against me."

"I don't understand," Dacari says, stepping away from her father's side. "I thought all the legends say that Chartreuse can't hurt or charm women?" Hunching her shoulders, Dacari's puzzled glare bounces around the room.

"Well actually the legend only states that she can't kill women. It doesn't say anything about charming women." Jackson replies as he moves away from the wall. "Lady Helsing, where are you going with this?"

"Like Dacari, I thought for sure she couldn't hurt me, so all these years I felt somewhat safe around her. That's why the night when they found her knife on me, I ran away—to her. I thought if I could give her back the dagger, then maybe she'd protect me. But when I arrived at her place, I heard her talking to her ward, Declan. She admitted how she charmed my father to kill Jerrica. And while I figured as much, it was when she revealed that her assault on Jerrica was only the icing on the cake. Her plan B, if you will."

Jackson's eyes grow dark as he makes his way to the middle of the parlor. "Claudia, I don't understand. If her attack on Jerrica was only a secondary motivation, what was her primary plan?"

A heavy, gloom-ridden mood permeates the room as wary glances are shared between Brian, Dacari, Jackson and Decaux. Fidgeting with her fingers, I can tell even Claudia is hesitant to continue. Lifting her eyes to mine for reassurance, Claudia bites her bottom lip, but I tug her shoulder tight, motioning for her to proceed.

"Damina, my lord." Claudia's voice is hardly audible, but with a parlor full of supernaturals I am certain her words were heard. And with the darkened expressions covering both Dacari and Jackson's faces, I know they understood every syllable.

"What do you mean Damina?" Dacari grits her words as she uses her speed and is in front of us in a flash. It's the first time I've seen Dacari make any otherworldly gesture beyond recanting the ancient words that brought about our newest monsters. Even with my keen vision, I barely saw anything more than a bolt of lightning before she appeared before our eyes. Interesting.

"Yes, Claudia. Please explain," Jackson huffs, making his way to Dacari's side in front of us.

"Why don't we all calm down," Brian adds, now making his way next to me. Although Jackson snarls in reply, Brian keeps his sights fixed on Dacari and the white glints of electricity flashing in her eyes.

"Explain!" Dacari bites back.

Closing her eyes tight, with her fists knotted at her sides, Dacari leans her chin to her shoulder as if she's resisting her own will. I know the feeling. I've known it my entire life. It's her wolf. Chomping at the bit, begging for a release. I've never seen a tribrid before but witnessing just an ounce of Dacari Peyroux's power is a spectacle in of itself.

Still, there's one person in the room strangely quiet. Her father. Decaux.

Keeping himself in the corner near the window, I quickly dart my eyes in his direction, but like Brian, he keeps his attention on Dacari.

Heaving a hard sigh, Claudia grips my hand tight. "Well, I heard her tell Declan that she charmed someone named Allyson to do what needs to be done to ensure Damina invoked her vampiric curse. When I heard her admit she could charm a woman, I got as far away from her as I could. To be honest, I didn't think much of the harm she could bring to Damina because I figured she would be protected by you, Lord Nashoba or Dalcour. And frankly, I didn't know who Allyson was so none of it made sense. But when news spread of what Allyson did to your mother, Delia, I finally understood why Damina would invoke her vampiric curse. That's why I came back to the mansion when I did. I'm just so sorry I didn't come forward sooner. I wanted to say something, but I was wanted for the assault on Jerrica. I assumed no one would believe me."

"It's okay, Lady Helsing, we believe you now," Brian says with a reassuring pat on Claudia's shoulder.

"The hell it is!" Dacari lashes, shoving Brian's shoulder. "That murderous siren-singing bitch had Allyson kill my mother! My mother, Brian!"

"Yes, your very *alive* mother, my dear daughter," Decaux quietly counters as he slowly saunters to our huddle. Dacari's eyes flash again as she regards him, but he flickers his crimson eyes in return, settling her ire. "Remember, you arrived just in time, and healed Delia."

"You did? I didn't know," Claudia gasps, gazing up at me. "Why didn't you tell me, Mark?"

"To be honest, babe, that whole day was a blur. After Braelyn…" my eyes glass and I look away. Claudia takes my chin in her hand, offering me a small smile.

"We've kept Delia hidden," Brian offers, turning to Claudia. "Only the few of us in this room, Dalcour, and Dranoel know of this. Lord Nashoba was always convinced there was more to Allyson's attack on Delia, but we couldn't put our finger on it. And then there was the undead."

"I don't give a rat's ass about the undead!" Dacari snaps. "I want to know why that pre-historic heifer tried to kill my mother! Dad—care to enlighten us?" Whipping her head over her shoulder, she turns her full attention to Decaux. "Because it's obvious you don't need enlightening. You already knew—didn't you?"

"Only recently," Decaux protests with his palms raised. "Just as Claudia prepared herself to tell Lord Helsing that day did I hear her thoughts. Honestly, I only heard rumors of Chartreuse charming women. I never gave much credence to them. But then there was Tabitha. DeLuca always claimed that Chartreuse set a muse upon her years ago."

"I don't care about years ago, father! I care about here and now! Okay yes, my mother is alive and well—there's still my cousin. Damina. She doesn't know mom is alive. And she's out there. All alone. Craving blood. Cursed. And it's all Chartreuse's fault. Even worse, Damina has no idea."

A low grumbling sound roars through Jackson and his sun spun eyes flash bright. Turning toward the glass parlor doors, a deep snarl rips through him. "I think she knows now."

Bright flickers of electricity bolt through the room like lightning. Looking through the glass doors I see what looks like an outline of Damina's frame in the doorway. Again, blinding flashes of light illuminate the room. But this time when we look up, Damina is gone.

Coming Soon

It was more than a one night-stand for me. She may think she's getting away from me, but I'm not letting her go that easy. Or ever for that matter. I've never met anyone like her. I want for nothing than to lay the world at her feet. Instead, I need to find a way to help her clean up the mess she's made in the world. I'll stay by her side no matter what. Neither my role as a Beta wolf or her devil of a daddy will keep me from making myself a permanent fixture in not only her life, but her heart.

So let's see, in the last thirty days I found out I've got not one, not two, but three supernatural forces living in me. Fell head-over-heels for the first man I—um—well...we'll get to that later. Found out my father is like the equivalent to the devil, but somehow loves me like no one else ever has. Oh, and yeah...I created a whole new monster...the Undead. Now that I've unleashed a curse seeking to cover the world in darkness and death, I have my work cut out for me. But I think this time death may have met its match.

More from L.C. Son

Here are a few more books and short stories in the Beautiful Nightmare Universe:
<u>Books</u>
Beautiful Nightmare (Book One)
Hearts Eclipsed, A Beautiful Nightmare Novella
Awaken: Beautiful Nightmare (Book Two)
Untamed: A Beautiful Nightmare Story
One Winter's Kiss: A Beautiful Nightmare Story
<u>Coming Soon</u>
Breaking Curses: A Beautiful Nightmare Novella-Planned 2022
Broken Moon ~ Planned 2022
Beta Rising - Summer 2022
Beautifully Dark Things- Planned 2023
Fire Kissed & Fire Born Duet Planned 2023
Dawn of Descent: Beautiful Nightmare (Book Three) TBA

<u>Short Stories</u>
I AM NO WITCH: A Beautiful Nightmare Short Story
With Clipped Wings of Butterflies: A Beautiful Nightmare Short Story
With Hearts Like Fire: A Beautiful Nightmare Short Story

For more info on my books, visit: My Books & Short Stories - L. C. Son Books (lcsonbooks.com)
Remember leaving reviews makes you an MVP!!
Thank you!

About L.C. Son

Known for her Amazon Best Selling Short Story, *With Hearts Like Fire* and the series starter and epic fantasy novel, *Beautiful Nightmare (Book One)*, L.C. Son is the happy wife of more than twenty years to her high school sweetheart and the loving mom of three.

Growing up, she spent hours reading comic books she "borrowed" from her older brother which inspired her love for heroes and all things fantasy and paranormal. Much like the characters she adored, she lives a duplicitous life. By day she works tirelessly to champion the employment of persons with severe disabilities. By night, she puts on her wife-mom cape, sharing with her husband at their church and juggling their kid's highly active schedules. Presently, she's working on the next installment in the Beautiful Nightmare series.

For the latest info and to join the member-only newsletter visit: www.lcsonbooks.com.
  Or use this link: https://linktr.ee/l.c.son